# The Adventures of
# Dougal

# The Adventures of Dougal

## Eric Thompson

Based on stories of *The Magic Roundabout*
by Serge Danot

Illustrations by David Barnett

BLOOMSBURY

*Eric Thompson was the creator of the scripts for the BBC TV Magic Roundabout series and the voice behind the characters. This omnibus edition comprises a selection of his stories which first appeared in:*

THE ADVENTURES OF DOUGAL *(First published 1971)*
DOUGAL'S SCOTTISH HOLIDAY *(First published 1971)*
THE MISADVENTURES OF DOUGAL *(First published 1972)*
DOUGAL ROUND THE WORLD *(First published 1972)*

*The characters in these stories which appear in the Magic Roundabout films were orginally created by Serge Danot for ORTF in a series entitled* Le Manége Enchanté.

This edition first published in 1998 by
Bloomsbury Publishing Plc

Bloomsbury Publishing Plc, 38 Soho Square, London W1V 5DF

A CIP catalogue record of this book is available from the
British Library

ISBN 0 7475 3806 9

10 9 8 7 6 5

Typeset by Dorchester Typesetting Group Ltd
Printed in Great Britain by Clays Ltd, St Ives plc

For his grandson, Ernie

# *Introduction*

We have dedicated this book to Ernie James Lumsden, the author's first grandchild, aged one as we write, and already reading in the bath. His grandfather did this too, but it must be admitted that he was never much interested in reading to his two daughters. The trouble was that his daughters really *wanted* him to read to them because he had a particularly lovely voice and smelt very comforting. They would choose *Pigling Bland* which had lots of words in it, but he insisted on *Miss Moppet* which had exquisite pictures but about three words on each page. Obviously this bred a great deal of resentment which he ignored.

When the BBC asked him to write *The Magic Roundabout* they lent him a machine with a tiny screen which he used to work with his feet. He watched the pictures without sound and wrote his script with a pencil and pad balanced on his knees. The stories had originally been written in French, but he didn't much like the French, so he changed it all – even the names, like Ermintrude the cow, who was inspired by his wife.

He thought Brian the snail was most like him – very optimistic and irritating. This was true, because before school in the morning when his daughters were still asleep he would appear in a revolting brown dressing-gown at their bedroom door and wake them by singing cheerfully:

Good morning, good morning,

We danced the whole night thru'.
Good morning, good morning to you.

This was very irritating indeed.

Once a lady wrote to him complaining that he used too many long words in *The Magic Roundabout* and how were children meant to understand them? He got out the *Oxford English Dictionary* and wrote back using all the longest and most difficult words he could find, like 'palimpsest' and 'oxymoron' (which sounds rude but isn't). He also wrote a strongly worded letter to a mother who had smacked her little boy for calling his sister a 'mollusc'.

He held serious conversations with babies in prams because he said they had to start somewhere. They were not to be patronised because they were little and hadn't lived as long as he had. All in all the author was quite badly behaved for his age. He hid chocolate all over the house and went to work in America just so that he could eat 'hot dogs' and 'knickerbocker glories'. His favourite food was fish and chips out of a newspaper, preferably the *Daily Mail* of which he did not approve. He preferred *The Times* but only for the crossword. He would have given Ernie a passion for cricket and football and might even have lent him his golf clubs. He would certainly have taken him fishing in Scotland and taught him to find 'docken-grubs' and worms for bait. He would have woken him up in the middle of the night, when the river was swelling with torrential rain and taken him out to dig up worms and talk to toads who were doing the same. On frosty nights they would have lain on their backs with binoculars and looked at the stars.

He had a country boy's wicked eye for a bird's nest and the glinting back of a water rat or an otter. He reared a family of 'hedgepigs' in his London garden but he didn't approve of dogs in town so he had a cat called Boot and a canary called Buxton. His favourite film stars were Clint Eastwood, Buster Keaton and Tom and Jerry.

We think he would have read to his grandson any hour of the day or night. Probably Dickens. It's a pity he can't, but at least Ernie will have his books.

Phyllida, Emma and Sophie Thompson
February 1998

# The Adventures of
# *Dougal*

# *Contents*

# Dougal and the Missing Link

Dougal was in bed thinking about not being in bed.

'To rise or not to rise, that is the question,' he mused.

'Good morning, Gossamer,' said Brian, arriving, as snails do, completely silently.

'I didn't hear you knock,' said Dougal, icily.

'I never knock,' said Brian, 'because I am a welcome visitor.'

'I've got news for you,' said Dougal. 'You

are about as welcome as a choc-ice to an Eskimo.'

'But I have things to tell,' said Brian. 'I am the bearer of tidings. I am the fleet-footed messenger of the garden.'

'You are a noisy mollusc,' said Dougal, 'but now you're here I suppose I'd better know what it's all about.'

And while Dougal made himself a cup of tea Brian told him the news. Zebedee hadn't been seen for some time. He wasn't answering his telephone or opening the door when it was knocked . . .

'IF it was knocked,' interrupted Dougal.

'Don't interrupt, old fruit-gum,' said Brian.

. . . and Zebedee wasn't collecting his milk and comics from the door-step.

'So Florence sent me to get you,' said Brian, 'because you would know exactly what to do . . . she said.'

'Naturally I know,' said Dougal, loftily.

'Come.' And they went.

Florence was waiting at Zebedee's house.

'I'm very worried,' she said. 'I've knocked, but there's no answer and no one's seen him anywhere else so he must be here.'

Dougal considered the case.

'He's nowhere else so he must be here,' he said. 'He doesn't answer the door so he *can't* be here and if he's not anywhere else and he's not here he must be . . . er . . .'

He took a short turn round a tree and back again.

'I'll have to start again,' he said. 'He's nowhere else so . . .'

Brian interrupted.

'Why don't we look inside?' he said. 'He may have left a farewell note.'

'There's no need to get dramatic,' said Dougal, 'but

there may be something in what you say.' And he backed off several paces.

'What are you doing, old thinker?' said Brian.

'I am going to rush at the door and break it down,' said Dougal.

'Oh, I see,' said Brian.

'Any objections?' said Dougal.

'Only one,' said Brian.

'Name it,' said Dougal.

'The door might not be locked,' said Brian.

Florence tried it. It wasn't.

'You could have done yourself an injury there,' said Brian, going in.

Inside, Zebedee's house was dark.

'Hello!' called Florence. 'Anyone home?'

There was a little

groan from the bed.

'Go away,' said A Voice, 'I am not receiving today.'

Now if someone groans and tells you to go away for some reason you always go nearer and Florence and Dougal and Brian did go nearer.

'Go away,' said the Voice again, and they went nearer still.

'Good heavens,' said Florence.

'Good heavens,' said Dougal.

'Fancy,' said Brian.

It was Zebedee. He was lying in bed with his hands over his face and looking very sad and odd.

'You look very sad,' said Florence.

'And odd,' said Dougal.

'Sad and odd,' said Brian.

'I am sad because I look odd,' said Zebedee, 'and I look odd because . . .'

Zebedee took his hands away from his face.

'Good gracious,' said Florence.

'Good heavens,' said Dougal.

'Fancy,' said Brian.

Zebedee had no moustache.

'That was a close shave,' said Dougal, giggling.

'Hush, Dougal,' said Florence, and she asked Zebedee what had happened.

'My moustache has been stolen,' said Zebedee.

'Barefaced robbery,' said Dougal, giggling again.

'Will you hush, Dougal,' said Florence, severely, and with Dougal hushed Zebedee told the story.

'It is not generally known,' he said, 'that my moustache is a false one. Not only that, it is a magic one. If it gets into the wrong hands disaster may befall us all. The situation is dire. Woe! Oh, woe!'

'He's going on a bit, isn't he?,' whispered Dougal.

'Just a whisker dramatic perhaps,' said Brian.

But Florence realised the seriousness of the situation.

'We will find it,' she cried. 'Don't worry. Come on, you two.'

They left Zebedee lying in bed making little groaning noises and went in search of the stolen moustache.

'We'll go in all directions and look for clues,' said Florence, 'and then we'll meet back here at tea-time. Now hurry, and mind you find it.'

'All right, bossy boots,' said Dougal.

'We will do our best,' said Brian. 'DOB! DOB! DOB!'

'DOB, DOB, DOB?!!' said Dougal. 'What are you on about, you pathetic little clump?'

'If you don't know, old scout, I'm not saying,' said Brian, sniggering, and he sped away.

'Hurry, Dougal,' said Florence, also speeding off.

'I am hurrying,' said Dougal, and he sat down under a tree to think.

'CAW! CAW!' said a voice.

'What!? What!? What!?' said Dougal. 'What!?'

'CAW!! CAW!!' said the voice again.

Dougal looked round and then up. On the topmost branch of the tree was a crow.

'CAW! CAW!' it said.

'You're making a lot of noise,' said Dougal, 'and your moustache is slipping.' He sat down again to think.

'The things you see,' he mused. 'A crow with a moustache.

A MOUSTACHE!!!!'

Dougal leapt to his feet and ran round the tree

eight times.

'Come down, you thief!' he screeched.

'Crows don't have moustaches! You've stolen it! Come down!'

'CAW! CAW!' said the crow. 'CAW!'

'I'll count to three,' said Dougal, 'and then if you don't come down, I'll come up.'

The crow looked at him.

'HAW!' it said.

Dougal was furious. He looked at the crow and he looked at the tree.

'All right, my friend,' he said grimly. 'You have raised the fighting spirit of the Clan Dougal. Be prepared to accept the quincequonces . . .'

And he started to climb.

Now dogs don't normally climb trees, but Dougal was no normal dog. He got one paw on a low branch and hauled himself up the tree trunk until his back legs were about two inches off the ground.

'So far so good,' he thought.

He got his other front paw over the branch and with a shivering heave he pulled himself up and stood on it.

'The important thing is not to look down,' he thought.

He looked down and nearly fell off.

The height was fearsome.

'Steady, Dougal,' he muttered. 'Steady. Be brave. Pretend you're a cat . . . What am I *saying*!'

He went on up. Not much like a cat – more like a dog trying to be a cat and not enjoying it very much, but he finally reached a branch just below where the crow was sitting.

'Got you!' panted Dougal.

'Give in and we'll say no more about it.'

The crow looked at him.

'CAW!' it said, and flew off.

Dougal sat wobbling on his branch.

'I suppose it should have occurred to me that crow might fly away,' he thought. 'I suppose I should have considered that possibility. I suppose I should have stopped to think. I suppose I'm stuck here for ever now.' And he gave a little wail.

Florence and Brian arrived back.

'Dougal's not here yet,' said Florence. 'I hope he's not lost himself.'

'I expect he has, great shaggy thing,' said Brian.

'I heard that!' shouted Dougal, 'You wait!'

They looked up.

'Dougal, you're up a tree!' said Florence.

'Do you know you're up a tree?' said Brian.

'Of course I know I'm up a tree,' said Dougal. 'I am not entirely without a sense of direction.'

'How did you get up a tree?' said Florence.

'Yes, how did you get up a tree?' said Brian.

'I flew,' said Dougal, sarcastically.

'Well, come down,' said Florence, 'because we have something to show you.'

'It's all very well saying "Come down",' said Dougal, 'but it's easier said than done, you know.'

'Skip lightly from branch to branch,' shouted Brian.

'I'll skip lightly all over you when I get down,' screeched Dougal.

Florence and Brian consulted together.

'Perhaps shaking the tree a little might dislodge him,' suggested Brian.

Florence was doubtful.

'I don't think he wants to be *dislodged* exactly,' she said, 'more *eased* down.'

'Will you two stop muttering and do something!' shouted Dougal. 'There's a nest up here and two birds in it are giving me very funny looks. Aahh!! Now they're offering me a worm!! Eugh!! Aahh!! Aaaaaaaa . . .'

There was a long wailing cry and Dougal arrived on the ground beside Florence and Brian.

'Right!' said Florence, briskly, 'Now you've finished being a bird perhaps we can get on.'

'Typical!' said Dougal. '*Typ-i-cal!* I risk life and limb and that's all the thanks I get.'

'We were supposed to be looking for Zebedee's moustache, not climbing trees,' said Florence. 'Anyway we've found it. A crow gave it to us.'

'Awfully nice crow,' said Brian . . . 'Said "CAW" a lot though.'

'I know the one,' said Dougal, heavily. 'An evil, beady creature.'

'He spoke very highly of you,' said Brian.

They went back into Zebedee's house and gave him his moustache.

'I am pathetically grateful,' he said, as he put it on, 'and to prove it I will provide delights.'

He muttered a few magic words and a magnificent feast appeared. Tomato and cucumber sandwiches for Florence, lettuce and carrot sandwiches for Brian, a huge pot of tea with sugar for Dougal, and a large plate of buns for everybody. They ate and ate.

'Tell me, old matey,' said Brian, sitting back rather full. 'Why were you up that tree?'

'I would rather not discuss it,' said Dougal. 'And pass me another bun.'

'You've had four,' said Brian.

'So who's counting?' said Dougal.

# *Dougal and a Mystery*

'Arise, Sir Dougal,' said the Queen.

Dougal arose.

'Hurrah for Dougal!' shouted a huge crowd of spectators.

Dougal bowed.

'Dougal for Prime Minister,' everyone roared.

Dougal waved a paw.

'Wake up, Dougal,' said Florence.

Dougal woke up.

'You are rotten,' he said. 'I was having a particularly lovely dream.'

'What about?' said Florence.

'What about?' said Dougal. 'Oh, this and that . . . er . . . nothing much. Is it time to get up?'

'It's been time to get up for *hours*,' said Florence. 'The birds have been awake for ages.'

'That's their problem,' said Dougal, reaching for the kettle. 'Would you like a cup of tea? I'm having one. And a biccy.'

He made Florence a cup of tea and she told him there was a problem in the garden.

'I never knew this place when it didn't have a problem,' said Dougal.

'But this is serious,' said Florence, sipping daintily. 'It's about the flowers.'

'Tell me all,' said Dougal. 'Want some toast?'

'I'm not sure we have time for toast,' said Florence.

Dougal paled.

'No time for toast?' he said. 'Nothing's that serious,' and he put some toast in the toaster.

'Time and toast wait for no man,' he giggled.

'Now, Dougal, you must be serious and listen,' said Florence.

'Marmalade?' said Dougal.

'Thank you,' said Florence.

'Sungwuns in itting uller lours,' she said.

'I beg your pardon?' said Dougal.

'Sungwuns in itting uller lours,' said Florence.

'You are very difficult to understand with your mouth full,' said Dougal. 'Would you care to start again?'

'Sorry,' said Florence, swallowing. 'I said "Someone's been eating all the flowers".'

Dougal tried to look concerned and failed.

'You don't seem very concerned,' said Florence.

'Oh, I am! I am!' said Dougal. 'I love flowers. I have marigolds in my window-box. Look!'

Florence looked.

'You haven't,' she said.

Dougal looked.

His marigolds were no longer there.

'What!!' he screeched. 'What!! What! What! How dare they! The vandals! The cads! The marigold munchers! After them! Track them down! Don't sit there eating toast. How can you eat toast with the garden crumbling about you? To arms! London's burning! The dam has burst!'

'Dougal,' said Florence, 'don't get confused.'

'Confused?!' said Dougal. 'I'm not confused. I'm just covering every possibility. Oh, put that toast down and come on!!'

Florence got up.

'Come along then,' she said. 'We'll go and investigate.'

They went out.

'Wait!' said Dougal, going back in.

Florence waited. Dougal came back. He was wearing a long cape, a deerstalker hat and smoking a large bendy pipe.

'Might as well do it properly,' he said. 'Come, Watson.'

'Watson?' murmured Florence.

They looked at the evidence. Dougal's marigolds had all gone, even the stalks, and as far as the eye could see there was not one flower.

'It may be an International Gang,' said Dougal. 'Have you been in touch with Interpol?'

'I thought I'd better come to you first,' said Florence.

'Very wise,' said Dougal, 'very wise.' And he nodded his head wisely.

'Your hat's falling off,' said Florence.

'I know,' said Dougal, coldly, putting it back on.

They ranged farther. Here and there was a trampled tulip or a bruised bluebell to show that something or someone had passed that way, but there wasn't a single flower standing proud.

They went on. Suddenly they came upon something odd. A small clearing in the garden which had normally been full of flowers was now empty except for a patch of yellow ones in the middle.

'How extraordinary,' said Florence, 'they've left some.'

'What are they?' said Dougal.

Florence inspected them. 'Cowslips,' she said.

'Oh, are they!' said Dougal, darkly. 'Oh, are they indeed? Oh, are they!!'

'Yes, they are,' said Florence.

'Are they indeed!' said Dougal. 'Ho! Ho! Are they?!'

Florence was a bit bewildered.

'Don't keep saying that, Dougal. They're just cowslips.'

'Doesn't that suggest anything to you?' said Dougal. 'Doesn't your little brain click at that fact? Cowslips. Why don't they eat cowslips?'

'Perhaps they don't like them,' said Florence.

Dougal smiled. 'You'll see,' he said.

Suddenly he pounced on something.

'Ah! Ha!' he screeched.

Florence jumped.

'Ah! Ha!' said Dougal again. 'We're on to them! Look!'

Florence looked. In a little patch of bare earth was a footprint.

'I might have known,' said Dougal. 'I might have known. Come on, quick, before she gets away.'

He raced on and Florence followed.

Dougal's nose was so close to the ground his pipe kept catching in the grass, but he finally skittered to a halt behind a tree and peered round.

'Look!' he said.

And Florence, panting, looked.

It was Ermintrude.

She was munching away at a patch of primroses and beside her, eating daisies, was another cow, wearing a trilby hat.

'A herd!' said Dougal. 'We'll need help. Call the Lone Ranger.'

'Don't be silly, Dougal,' said Florence, 'it's only Ermintrude.'

'What about her friend?' said Dougal. 'She looks a bit deadly.'

Florence started forward.

'Where are you going?' said Dougal, in a panic.

'I'm going to have a word with them,' said Florence, 'and tell them to stop eating the flowers.'

'Careful,' said Dougal, 'they may charge.'

'Nonsense,' said Florence, and she went.

'Hello, dear thing,' said Ermintrude.

'How are you? And how's your little furry friend Donald?'

'Dougal!!!' screeched Dougal. 'I'm called Dougal! And I'm not little and furry!'

'Well, you're not big and bald, are you darling?' said Ermintrude. 'But we won't quibble. I'd like to introduce my friend Janice. She's paying me a visit, so I'm showing her round.'

Florence said hello to Janice.

'Dashed pleased to meet you,' boomed Janice. 'Ermy told me all about you. Been wantin' to visit for a long time. Nice little place you've got here. Very sportin' country.'

'Tell them about the flowers,' hissed Dougal.

'What's that hissin'?' said Janice.

'It's nothing,' said Florence, quickly. 'Er . . . Ermintrude, may I have a word with you?'

'Of course, dear thing,' said Ermintrude. 'As many as you like.'

'Well,' said Florence, leading her to one side. 'I don't want to seem unkind, especially as you have your friend with you, but it is a rule that we don't eat the flowers in this garden.'

'It's a strict rule,' said Dougal, 'and it applies to *all*.'

Ermintrude looked very abashed.

'My dears, I don't know *what* to say,' she mooed. 'I'm covered in confusion.'

'And primrose juice,' muttered Dougal.

'Janice, my dear, we've been very naughty,' said Ermintrude.

Janice looked startled.

'Eh?' she said.

'We've eaten Forbidden Fruit,' said Ermintrude.

'And forbidden primroses,' said Dougal, 'not to mention buttercups, daisies and MY marigolds.'

Ermintrude and Janice were very contrite when they realised just how much of the garden they had lain bare.

'Don't know our own capacity, old thing,' said Janice.

'Got carried away,' said Ermintrude.

Florence told them that they mustn't get carried away again and that from now on the flowers must not be eaten.

'But you can have as much grass as you like,' she said.

'Hate grass,' said Janice.

'Hush, dear,' said Ermintrude, and she promised Florence that they would be good in future, however strong the temptation.

'That's splendid,' said Florence, 'and now we'll all go back to Dougal's house for a cup of tea.'

'I beg your pardon?' said Dougal, going quite pale.

'We're coming to tea,' said Florence, 'at your place.'

'But I haven't got a thing in!' said Dougal. 'I'm not prepared. There's not a cake baked or a biccy in the tin.'

'We don't want biscuits, silly boy,' said Ermintrude. 'We'll just pick a few flowers on the way.'

And she laughed.

'Ermintrude, you're dreadful,' said Florence.

'I know, dear,' said Ermintrude.

# *Dougal and the Garden Navy*

Dougal was up and about. It was a bright, sunny morning and he was just finishing his seventh cup of tea and his fourteenth biscuit when he heard shouting outside.

'Now what?' he thought, pouring another cup.

The shouting got louder and there were other noises too; something that sounded like a drum and something that sounded like nothing on earth.

'Obviously an anti-Government riot,' thought Dougal, pouring another cup of tea. 'I will not get involved.'

BANG! BANG! BANG!

Dougal leapt about four feet in the air; something was banging on his door.

CRASH! CRASH! CRASH!

Dougal leapt again as the door quivered.

'Come out, Dougal!' shouted a voice.

Dougal was furious.

'They can't do this to me!' he screeched.

They could.

BANG! CRASH! Come out Dougal!

Dougal opened the door just as Florence was about to bang on it again with a large megaphone.

'I wouldn't do that if I were you,' said Dougal, quietly.

'Oh, good, Dougal, you're awake,' said Florence.

'Awake?' said Dougal. 'I'll never be able to sleep again! What's the meaning of all this?'

He looked around.

There was Florence dressed in a pith helmet and sailor suit which was rather too big for her.

There was Brian with flags flying from both horns.

There was Dylan in bell-bottom trousers playing a set of bagpipes.

There was Mr Rusty banging a drum and there was Ermintrude wearing a sailor hat with 'KISS ME QUICK' written on it.

'I take it you've all gone dotty,' said Dougal. 'Well, it had to happen sooner or later.'

'It's Navy Day, old admiral,' said Brian, 'and we are going to launch our boat. You are in command and I'm chief mutineer. Yo! Ho! Ho! and a bottle of carrot juice.'

'He's right,' said Florence. 'You are the only one for captain and we've brought you the captain's hat.'

She showed him. It was a marvellous hat covered in gold braid.

Dougal tried not to seem too pleased,

'I'd better humour you all, I suppose,' he said, putting on the hat which was only a little too big for him. 'Where is this fighting vessel?'

'Over there!' they said.

'Lead on!' they said.

'Strike the drum!' they said.

Dougal took the megaphone from Florence and tied it under his chin.

'Keep in step!' he shouted. 'No talking in the ranks! Remember Nelson!'

And the procession moved off. Two small birds sitting on a fence watched them.

'Is it the Revolution?' said one.

'If it is, it's failed,' said the other.

The procession went on, Dylan playing his bagpipes hopefully, Mr Rusty banging the drum, and Brian singing a sea shanty and occasionally letting out a piercing whistle.

'Isn't it exciting?' breathed Florence.

'If you can stand the noise,' said Dougal. 'How much farther to the sea?'

'Oh, we're not going to the sea,' said Florence, 'we're going to Mr MacHenry's.'

Dougal stopped, and the procession piled up behind him with a bump, bump, bump.

'Mr MacHenry's!?' he said. 'I thought we were going

to launch a boat?'

'So we are,' they said.

'But Mr MacHenry doesn't live by the sea,' said Dougal, 'so how can we launch a boat?'

'Oh, don't quibble!' they said. 'Captains shouldn't quibble. On! On!'

And the procession moved on.

Two rabbits sitting in a field watched them.

'Is it the Revolution?' said one.

'Must be,' said the other.

The procession arrived at Mr MacHenry's, and he was there to meet them wearing an admiral's hat.

'Glad you could all come,' he said. 'At ease, and we'll get on with it.'

Dougal sat down firmly.

'Now just a moment,' he said.

'We wait! We wait!' sang Brian.

'Quiet!' said Dougal.

'Quiet! Quiet!' shouted Brian. 'All be quiet!! QUIET!!!'

'You're the only one making a noise,' said Dougal.

'Sorry, old matelot,' said Brian.

'I want a few things cleared up,' said Dougal, 'before we go any further. One, I have been invited to a nautical venture, right?

'Right,' they said.

'I am to be the captain of a boat, right?'

'Right,' they said.

'The boat is somewhere here, right?'

'Right,' they said.

'But this is not the sea, right?'

'Right,' they said.

'So a boat won't be any use, right?'

'Wrong,' they said. 'Come and see.'

And there, in Mr MacHenry's field, was the boat. It had masts, a funnel, two anchors and a rudder to steer with.

'Isn't it marvellous?' breathed Florence.

Dougal went cautiously to inspect his new command.

'Wait a moment, Captain Sir!' said Brian, 'and we'll pipe you on board.'

Everyone except Dougal went on board and waited. Brian said 'GO!' and Dylan played his bagpipes while Dougal walked slowly up the gang-plank.

'A very moving ceremony,' said Mr Rusty.

'It's about the only thing likely to move in this Navy,' said Dougal, 'so be quiet and listen.'

'Quiet! Quiet!' shouted Brian. 'All be quiet! QUIET!!!'

'You can't imagine how annoying that is,' said Dougal.

'Sorry, old tug-boat,' said Brian.

Dougal assumed an attitude of importance on the bridge.

'Crew members,' he said, 'listen carefully . . .'

'QUIET!!!' shouted Brian.

'If you do that once more I shall not be responsible for my actions,' said Dougal.

'Sorry,' said Brian.

'Now,' said Dougal, 'far be it from me to stifle the spirit of enterprise, but I feel I must point out that this boat, in common with other boats, does need water to make it go. We have no water, therefore it won't go. I would welcome suggestions.'

He looked round.

'We thought perhaps you could push it, old mariner,' said Brian.

Dougal looked at him so hard that Brian had to go into his shell to recover.

'Any *other* suggestions?' asked Dougal.

'I think we'd better call Zebedee,' said Florence, and she did.

When Zebedee arrived he found the Garden Navy in a sad state. They explained the problem to him – how they had a boat but no water – and asked if he could help.

'As I see it,' said Zebedee, 'there are two alternatives. We either get the boat to the water or the water to the boat. Getting the boat to the water will take time, and getting the water to the boat will take a miracle, so . . .

He paused and looked at the boat.

'Perhaps a third alternative . . .'

And he muttered a word or two.

PING! PING! PING! PING!

'There you are,' he said, and he left.

They looked round. Nothing seemed to have changed.

'Nothing's changed,' said Dougal. 'What did he do?'

They rushed from side to side looking about them and as they did so the boat moved a little – then a little more.

'It's moving!' said Florence.

They stopped rushing from side to side and the boat stopped moving.

'It's . . . like . . . stopped,' said Dylan.

'Rush about!' said Brian, and they rushed.

The boat moved.

'Stop rushing!' said Brian, and they stopped.

The boat stopped.
They looked over the side.
It's got wheels!' they shrieked. 'Hurrah!!'

Dougal looked very upset.
'My first command,' he said, 'a boat with wheels. I'll never live it down in Pompey.'
'Stop moping,' said Florence, 'we must get under way.'
'And how do you propose getting under way, bossy boots?' said Dougal. 'We may have wheels but we don't have an engine.'
'You're right,' said Florence.
'He's right,' said Brian.

'Unfortunately,' said Mr MacHenry.

'It's simple,' said Dylan, 'we need a pull or a push,' and he dropped off to sleep.

'Exactly,' said Mr Rusty, 'a pull or a push.'

'Any volunteers,' said Dougal, 'to pull or push?'

They all looked at him.

'Er . . . who's going to volunteer?' said Dougal again.

They looked at him harder.

'You're a rotten lot,' said Dougal.

'You're the captain,' they said, 'it's up to you to keep the ship sailing.'

'It's a captain's duty,' said Florence.

'And you're the captain,' said Brian.

So Dougal, wishing he'd never been elected captain, went over the side, took hold of a rope, and began to pull.

'We're moooving,' said Ermintrude.

'At last!' said Florence.

'Rotters!' panted Dougal.

The Garden Navy moved slowly along. No one knew quite where it was going and no one, except Dougal, seemed to care. Brian organised a sing-song on board while Florence prepared tea and cakes in the galley.

'Whose turn next to pull?' panted Dougal.

'You're the captain,' they said, heartlessly.

But suddenly Dougal found that the pulling had got a little easier. He let go of the rope and the boat continued to move. It was going downhill and beginning to pick up speed.

'Whee!!' they all said on board. 'Whee!! Wheeee!!!'

The hill got steeper and the boat went faster.

Dougal ran alongside . . .

'Er . . . excuse me,' he shouted.

'You're the captain,' they laughed.

'All right then,' said Dougal, and he sat down and watched.

The boat went faster down the hill. As it bumped along cakes and cups from the tea-party fell overboard, Dougal picked up the cakes and followed slowly.

'You can stop now!!' they shrieked.

'I feel sick,' moaned Brian.

'Look ahead,' quavered Mr Rusty.

Ahead there was a gleam. It was the sun shining on water. The Garden Navy was about to launch itself and Dougal, his mouth full of cake, watched and waited.

The boat hit the water with a great splash, shot out into the middle of the pond and sank. Luckily the water was very shallow and the boat settled on the bottom leaving the deck sticking up out of the water.

'Enjoying yourselves?' shouted Dougal from the bank. 'Having a good sail? Missing your captain?'

He chortled and ate another cake.

On board the crew felt very sorry for themselves.

'Scuppered,' said Brian, mournfully.

'Sunk without trace,' said Ermintrude, inaccurately.

'We'll have to wade ashore,' said Florence, apprehensively.

'I can't wade, I'm legless,' wailed Brian.

'I'll carry you, snaily dear,' said Ermintrude.

'Too kind,' murmured Brian.

So they came ashore, all wet and muddy.

'A fine looking crew!' said Dougal. 'What are you?'

'A fine looking crew,' they said, sadly.

'Oh, come on,' said Dougal, 'you'd better come back to my place for baths and a cup of tea.'

'Oh, you are good to us, Captain Sir,' said Brian.

'Don't push your luck,' said Dougal.

# Dougal, RSPCA

Dougal was fast asleep and dreaming, as usual, of glory. He dreamed he was leading a charge against a castle belonging to a particularly wicked giant. The giant was holding Florence prisoner in durance vile and Dougal was rescuing her. He struggled doggedly by the hill whilst the giant's cannon thundered from the battlements and cannonballs whistled about his ears.

BANG! BANG! BANG! went the cannon.

'On! On!' shouted Dougal.

BANG! BANG! BANG!

'On! On!'

BANG! BANG! BANG!

Dougal was suddenly awake but the guns were still going.

BANG! BANG! BANG!

It was someone knocking at his door.

'Really,' said Dougal. 'How rotten.'

BANG! BANG! BANG! went the door.

'All right! All right! I'm coming!'

shouted Dougal, and he heaved out of bed and opened the door.

There was no one there.

'What!?' said Dougal.

'What?! I thought someone was knocking?'

'Someone was,' said a voice. 'It was me.'

Dougal looked round.

'Who's me?' he said.

'Up here,' said the voice somewhere over his head.

Dougal looked up.

It was a butterfly.

'Was that you knocking?' he said.

'Who else?' said the butterfly. 'May I come in?'

'I think you'd better,' said Dougal, so the butterfly came in and settled on the back of a chair.

'Nice little place you've got here,' it said.

'Thank you,' said Dougal, putting on the kettle. 'Want some tea?'

The butterfly looked a little pained.

'Butterflies don't drink tea,' it said, 'but I'd appreciate a sip of nectar.'

'You sure you wouldn't prefer ambrosia?' said Dougal, sarcastically.

'Butterflies never touch ambrosia,' said the butterfly,

'I thought everyone knew that.'

'Of course,' said Dougal, 'silly of me.'

The butterfly made itself at home, opening and closing its wings and whistling 'Tea for Two' as Dougal bustled about.

'Er . . . have you called for any particular reason, Miss . . . ?' said Dougal.

'Mister,' said the butterfly, tersely.

Dougal blushed.

'Oh, I am sorry, I thought you were a lady,' he said.

'I don't know what you're implying,' said the butterfly, 'but the name's Stokeley, and I want you to sign my petition.'

'Petition?' said Dougal.

'Against butterfly-hunting,' said Stokeley. 'It's a cruel sport and I'm organising a petition against it.'

Dougal choked on his tea and pushed his butterfly net under the sofa with his paw.

'Of course I'll sign,' he said, hurriedly.

There was another knock on the door, and Florence and Brian came in with butterfly nets.

'Ready to go?' said Florence.

'All geared up?' said Brian.

'What are you talking about?' said Dougal.

'Butterfly-hunting,' said Florence. 'It's today.'

Dougal leapt to his feet, making a loud clatter with his cup and saucer.

'Oh, yes!' he laughed. 'A joke! Ha! Ha!'

Brian and Florence looked puzzled.

'What *do* you mean?' they asked.

Dougal rushed about.

'Come on, old hunter, or we'll miss all the best ones,'

said Brian.

'Ha! Ha!' said Dougal, so loudly that Florence jumped. 'Yes! What a joke! May I introduce an . . . er . . . acquaintance of mine. Ha! Ha!'

Florence and Brian looked, saw the butterfly and tried to hide their nets behind them.

'Name's Stokeley,' said the butterfly, slowly.

'I'm Florence,' said Florence, blushing.

'And I'm Brian,' said Brian, blushing even more than Florence.

'And where did you say you were going?' said Stokeley, *very* slowly.

'Er . . . butterscotch shunting,' said Brian in rather a high-pitched voice.

'It's . . . er . . . a new game . . . played with . . . er nets and . . . er . . . butterscotch.'

Stokeley fluttered his wings, and looked at them extremely hard.

Florence was very ashamed.

'I feel very ashamed,' she said. 'We're not telling the truth. We were going chasing butterflies, but I didn't realise anyone felt strongly about it.'

'Butterflies feel very strongly about it,' said Stokeley.

'I think we'd better all have a cup of tea,' said Dougal.

'Got any carrot juice?' said Brian.

'You'll have tea and like it,' said Dougal.

'I'll have it, but I won't like it,' said Brian.

They all settled down and Stokeley explained about his petition. As he said, butterflies were used to being chased and he had himself sometimes quite enjoyed it, but it had now got out of hand and must be stopped.

'It's come to a pretty pass when you can't enjoy a

good flower in peace without something creeping up behind you,' he said, and they agreed.

'Butterflies are peace-loving creatures and shouldn't be chased,' he said, and they agreed.

'Butterflies add beauty to the world,' he said, and they agreed.

'So sign my petition,' he said, and they agreed, and signed.

Stokeley thanked them and said he'd better be on his way as he had a lot of people to call on.

Florence opened the door.

'Peace, peace!' said Stokeley, and he left.

'Well,' said Dougal. 'Anyone want another cup of tea?'

'No,' said Florence, firmly. 'I think we should go straight out and make sure no one is chasing any butter-flies. It's our duty.'

'It's our duty, old tea-urn,' said Brian.

'Oh, all right,' said Dougal. 'We'll go.'

So they went.

The garden was looking beautiful. The flowers were all in bloom, and here and there a butterfly was sipping nectar.

'Looks as though your friend has been successful,' said Brian, 'not a single chaser anywhere.'

'It's all so peaceful,' said Florence. 'So peaceful.'

'Aaah!' screeched Dougal. 'Look!'

They looked. There, some way away, was a figure. It was holding a net and creeping up on something.

'A butterfly-chaser!' said Florence.

'The vandal!' said Dougal.

'Let's leap on him!' said Brian.

But they were too late. The figure pounced with his

net and rushed off.

'After him!' shouted Dougal. 'Come on, men!'

'Men?' said Florence.

'Oh, don't quibble,' said Dougal, and he raced after the distant figure.

'What fun!' said Brian, from the top of Dougal's head.

Dougal screeched to a halt.

'What are you doing up there?' he demanded.

'Well, you don't expect me to run, do you?' said Brian. 'I am a snail, not a fox-hound.'

'Oh, stop arguing, you two, or he'll get away,' said Florence.

They followed fast and gradually caught up with the figure carrying the butterfly net.

'Good heavens,' said Florence, 'it's Mr MacHenry.'

And it was.

'Whoever would believe it?' said Brian.

'The cad!' said Dougal.

Mr MacHenry stopped and put the butterfly net down.

'What's he doing?' hissed Dougal.

'He's taking a rest,' said Brian.

'Now's our chance,' said Florence.

They crept up to the net. Inside, looking a little pale, was Stokeley.

'Come out,' said Dougal, 'while he's not looking.'

'I can't,' said Stokeley. 'I'm hooked up.'

'Leave this to me,' said Dougal, bravely, and he pushed his way into the net. Stokeley, unhooked, flew out and sat on Brian's shell, but before Dougal could get out Mr MacHenry picked up the net, put it over his shoulder, and left.

'Good heavens,' said Florence, 'whatever shall we do?'

'I think we should follow and observe,' said Brian.

'It might be fun.'

So they followed.

Dougal was in a bit of a quandary and a lot of discomfort.

He didn't dare make a noise or Mr MacHenry might drop the net, so he decided to wait and see.

'It's a far, far better thing,' he sighed.

The procession continued. Mr MacHenry with Dougal slung in a net over his shoulder; Florence, Brian and Stokeley at a discreet distance.

'I wonder where he's going,' said Florence.

She soon found out. Mr MacHenry stopped at his greenhouse, put down the net without looking at it and went in.

The others rushed up to Dougal.

'Are you all right?' they said.

'You mean apart from being in this net?' said Dougal, with heavy sarcasm.

'I don't think this is the time for sarcasm,' said Florence. 'I think you should get out.'

'How can I get out when I am totally enclosed in net?' said Dougal. 'Haven't you got any scissors?'

'Sorry, no,' said Florence.

'I could bite through it,' said Brian.

'And how long would that take?' said Dougal.

'About four days,' said Brian, 'if I hurried.'

'Look out!' said Stokeley. 'He's coming back.'

They rushed behind a bush and watched.

Mr MacHenry came out of the greenhouse, went to pick up the net, saw Dougal, and stopped.

'Good morning,' said Dougal.

'Er . . . good morning,' said Mr MacHenry.

'Lovely day,' said Dougal.

'Er . . . lovely,' said Mr MacHenry.

'Lost something?' said Dougal.

'Er . . . yes,' said Mr MacHenry.

He looked over his shoulder.

'Seize him!' shouted Dougal, and the others rushed out and seized him.

'What's going on?' said Mr MacHenry.

'You're being seized!' they said.

Mr MacHenry sat down.

'I surrender,' he said. 'And I demand an explanation.'

'We are the ones who demand an explanation,' said Dougal. 'What do you mean by catching butterflies? Explain!'

'Yes, explain!' said Stokeley, fluttering close to Mr MacHenry.

'Oh, I thought I recognised you,' said Mr MacHenry.

'Then explain!' they said.

So Mr MacHenry explained.

It was all very simple. He had lots of flowers in his greenhouse and he needed a few butterflies to eat the nectar.

'So I thought I'd catch some and bring them here,' he said.

'Why didn't you put a notice up?' said Stokeley.

'I didn't think butterflies could read,' said Mr MacHenry. 'Silly of me.'

Stokeley decided that Mr MacHenry had acted with the best intentions, so he forgave him and promised to visit every day with a few friends.

'You'll be very welcome,' said Mr MacHenry.

'All's well that ends well,' said Florence.

'And it was fun while it lasted,' said Brian.

'Perhaps you'd all join me for tea,' said Mr Mac-Henry, and they said they'd be delighted.

'Come along then,' said Mr MacHenry, and they went in and shut the door.

'What about me!' screeched Dougal.

Two butterflies flew past.

'What a shame,' said one. 'Fancy putting that poor creature in a net.'

'Oh, I don't know, Harold,' said the other. 'He looks a bit dangerous.'

Florence came out with some scissors.

'Sorry we forgot you, Dougal,' she said brightly, cutting him free, 'but we were having such a lovely time.'

'Good of you to bother,' said Dougal, sarcastically. 'I don't suppose there's any tea left.'

'We might find you a little something,' said Florence. 'Come along.'

# Dougal and the House Party

Dougal was sipping a cup of tea one morning and thinking about his house.

'I wonder if I should move,' he thought. 'Sell up the old homestead and seek pastures new?'

He looked around.

'It's getting a bit tatty,' he thought. 'One strong wind and it would all fall down.'

He sneezed; a picture fell off a hook, the window flew open and a cloud of soot fell down the chimney.

'That does it,' said Dougal, 'I'm leaving this place.'

He sneezed again. The carpet rolled up and a leg fell off a chair.

'I deserve better than this,' said Dougal. 'I should be provided for by the Government. I demand a subsidy.'

There was a knock on the door. Two cups fell off the dresser and Dougal's chair collapsed.

'Come in,' he said, heavily.

Brian came in.

'Why are you sitting on the floor, old thing?' he said.

'I would prefer,' said Dougal, getting up, 'if you would state your business and stop asking silly questions.'

'I say, you're in a bit of a pickle here, aren't you?' said Brian. 'Broken cups, broken chairs, soot everywhere . . .

been having a party?'

'Yes, I was entertaining a snail,' said Dougal.

'Oh, anyone I know?' said Brian.

'Oh, be quiet!' said Dougal.

He sat down heavily on another chair. It collapsed.

'You're sitting on the floor again,' said Brian.

Dougal groaned.

'It's too much!' he said. 'It's too much!'

'I can see you're upset,' said Brian. 'Tell your little mate *everything*.'

'If my little mate doesn't watch it, my little mate is going to find himself thumped,' said Dougal.

He got up.

'Look at it all,' he said. 'Not fit for a . . . a . . . snail to live in. I must move, make a fresh start.'

'I know what you want,' said Brian.

'What?' said Dougal. 'Apart from you out of here?'

'You want a fresh start,' said Brian. 'I will rally your chums and we will build you a new house. Leave it to me!' And he rushed out, slamming the door.

The bookcase fell down and the room filled with soot.

'I can't stand it,' said Dougal, sitting on the table.

It collapsed.

Brian found Florence talking to Dylan, Ermintrude and Mr Rusty.

'Oh, it's a lucky chance finding you all together,' he said, 'because we are needed by someone.'

'Who?' said Florence.

'Someone very dear to all of us,' said Brian. 'Our best friend.'

They all thought.

'We give up, man,' said Dylan. 'Who?'

'Shaggy breeks,' said Brian. 'My little hairy mate. That dog.'

'Dougal?' said Florence. 'What's the matter with him?'

'His house is falling about his ears,' said Brian, 'and I said we would build him another one.'

'That was a bit rash of you, dear thing,' said Ermintrude, 'because we don't know how to build a house.'

'Very tricky, house-building,' said Mr Rusty, pessimistically.

'It needs, like, expertise,' said Dylan. 'And bricks,' he added.

'But he needs it,' said Brian. 'Are we going to let him down?'

'Certainly not,' said Florence. 'We will do our best for our friend Dougal, won't we?'

'We will!' they said, 'We will do our best!'

'Our very, very best!' said Florence.

'Yes, indeed!' they said.

And having decided that their best was going to be done, they sat down to think about how to do it.

'We need plans,' said Brian, 'and wood and nails and doors and windows and furniture and carpets and cups and saucers and a tea-pot and a lot of lettuce.'

'Lettuce?' they said.

'Well, you don't want me to starve, do you?' said Brian.

'Why, what are you going to be doing?' they said.

'Supervising,' said Brian. 'Giving orders. Very taxing to the brain. And my first order is "Ready! Steady! Go!"'

So they went.

Meanwhile, back amongst the soot and broken furniture, Dougal was beginning to brighten up.

'I must not mope,' he said, firmly. 'Mope will get me nowhere. I must act.'

He looked amongst the books on the floor and found one called, luckily, HOW TO BUILD A HOUSE.

'Now that's very lucky,' he thought, and he settled down to read. Unfortunately, books on house-building aren't very easy to read and Dougal found his eyes getting heavier and heavier.

'I mustn't go to sleep,' he thought, going to sleep.

Florence and the others arrived at Dougal's house. They looked through the open window and saw Dougal asleep.

'Now's our chance,' said Florence. 'We'll build it before he wakes up and give him a surprise.'

'If we build it before he wakes up, I'll get the surprise,' said Brian.

'Now no defeatism,' said Florence. 'Remember you're in charge.'

Brian remembered.

'Right, let's get on with it,' he said.

Taking care not to step on Dougal, they took the house apart bit by bit until they had it all laid out and ready to put up again.

'I hope we remember where it all goes,' said Mr Rusty.

Ermintrude dropped a chimney pot.

'Sh!!' said Florence, 'you'll wake him.'

They decided to put Dougal's house together again a little way away from where Dougal was sleeping, and they set about it making as little noise as possible.

They got the walls up and stood back to look at it.

'I don't want to worry anyone,' said Dylan, 'but is it ... like ... exactly right?'

'No time to worry about that,' said Brian. 'Got to get the roof on.'

They got the roof on.

'Now for the furniture,' said Florence. 'Mend it carefully and bring it in.'

They mended it carefully, dusted it all off and put it in place.

'We've forgotten the drains,' said Brian. 'The water won't run out of his sink and you know what he's like – always making tea.'

This was a bit of a problem.

'Are you good at drains?' said Florence.

'Not particularly,' said Brian, 'but I know someone who is. I'll go and get him.'

So Brian went to get his friend while the others put the finishing touches to the house.

Florence ironed the curtains and put them up. Ermintrude beat the soot out of the carpet.

Dylan put the books in the bookcase and Mr Rusty got in everybody's way.

Brian came back.

'Here we are,' he said, 'my friend Frank. He's a mole

and very good at drains.'

'Afternoon all,' said Frank. 'Show me the problem.'

'We need drains for the sink,' they said.

'Easy,' said Frank, and he climbed into the sink and disappeared.

'Where's he gone?' said Florence, peering.

'I dread to think,' said Brian.

There was a shout from outside. There was Frank, covered in mud, sitting on the ground about twenty yards away.

'Far enough?' he called.

They went over.

'Have you done it?' said Florence.

'Of course,' said Frank. 'It's a great drain – one of my best.'

'What would we have done without you?' said Florence. 'Drains were our main problem.'

'It's nothing,' said Frank. 'People do get worried about drains, don't know why.'

And he disappeared.

'Good heavens,' said Florence, 'where's he gone now?'

'To catch the Underground, I expect,' said Mr Rusty, and he laughed so much he fell over.

They went back to the house. It did look a bit odd,

but as Florence said they *had* done it in a hurry.

'Shall we wake Dougal up?' said Ermintrude.

'No!' said Brian. 'Let's carry him in and put him to bed.'

'Oh, yes!' said Florence. 'What a surprise he'll get.'

Dylan looked at the house.

'You can say that again, man,' he said.

They tiptoed across to Dougal and picked him up.

'Which end have you got?' said Brian, puffing a lot.

'Does it matter?' said Florence.

They put Dougal into his bed and crept out.

'We'll come back later,' said Florence, 'at tea-time.'

'Won't he get a surprise?' they said.

'Aren't we clever?' they said.

And they left, closing the door behind them with a bang.

Dougal woke up, yawned and stretched.

'What a dream!' he thought. 'All about my house falling down and the furniture breaking. Funny.'

He got up.

'I'll just have a cup of tea,' he said, putting the kettle under the tap and turning it on.

'Here is the weather forecast,' said the tap.

'What?!' screeched Dougal.

'Here is the weather forecast,' said the tap again.

'I don't want the weather forecast, I want water!' shouted Dougal.

'Heavy rain is about to fall *everywhere*,' said the tap.

'Oh, shut up!' said Dougal, and he turned the tap off.

'Now what is going on?' he thought. 'Something's happened while I've been asleep. I wonder what?'

He turned on the television and a jet of water hit him in the eye.

'What?!' he screeched, mopping himself down.

'What?! What?! What?!'

He ran around in little circles to calm himself down.

'I must be calm,' he thought.

He went to the front door. It wouldn't open.

'Trapped!' he thought, rushing to the back door.

It wasn't there.

'Someone's stolen my back door!' shouted Dougal. 'Help! Vandals!'

He rushed upstairs. There was the back door in the bedroom wall. He opened it and went out.

'Ahh!!' he screamed, clinging on to the television aerial, 'Help! Help!'

Just then Florence and the others came back to see how Dougal was getting on in his new house.

'What's that noise?' said Mr Rusty.

'It's Dougal shouting for joy, I expect,' said Florence.

'Help! Help!' shouted Dougal.

'I don't think it's *joy* exactly,' said Brian. 'Look!'

They looked up. There was Dougal, ashen, clinging to his television aerial.

'What *are* you doing, Dougal?' said Florence.

'Come down at once.'

Dougal came down with a thud, bringing the aerial with him.

'We've come to tea,' said Florence. 'May we go in?'

Dougal groaned.

'Be my guests.' he said.

Florence tried the door. It wouldn't open.

'It won't

open,' she said. 'We'll have to go round to the back door.'

'The back door's up there!' screeched Dougal. 'Someone's trying to drive me mad!'

Florence looked.

'Oh, dear,' she said.

'Oh, dear,' said the others.

'Have we boobed?' said Brian.

'Oh, dear,' they said.

Dougal looked at them.

'Am I to understand,' he said slowly, 'that you are responsible for all this?'

'Sorry, old cabbage,' said Brian. 'We were trying to help.'

'Like . . . help,' said Dylan.

'We did our best,' said Mr Rusty.

'Sorry,' said Florence, and she called to Zebedee and explained the situation.

'I think I can do something about that,' said Zebedee, and he said a few magic words.

Dougal's house gave a creak and a thud, hopped a few feet in the air and came to rest in its old position.

'I think that'll be all right now,' he said, leaving.

Dougal opened the door and peered inside.

'Perhaps you'd all better come in for a cup of tea,' he said.

They went in. The house was beautiful. The back door was in its right position and everything was new and shining.

'Pleased, Dougal?' said Florence.

Dougal sat down carefully. The chair creaked.

'Time will tell,' he said.

# Dougal and the Perfumed Garden

Dougal was fast asleep when there was a tap on his door. The tap wasn't loud enough to wake him up at once, but it went on getting louder and louder until finally Dougal woke.

'What?!' he said. 'What! What! What!'

He grumbled out of bed, unlocked the door and opened it.

It was Brian.

'Yes?' said Dougal, icily.

'Hello,' said Brian. 'Er . . . how are you?'

Dougal looked at him hard.

'It is three o'clock in the morning,' he said, 'and I'm not very well.'

'Sorry to hear that,' said Brian, 'may I come in?'

And he came in.

'I expect you're wondering what I want?' he said, cheerfully.

'Nothing was further from my mind,' said Dougal, putting the kettle on, 'but I suppose I shall have to listen.'

'Well, it's very exciting really,' said Brian. 'There's a prowler in the garden.'

'A prowler? said Dougal. 'What's he doing?'

'Prowling,' said Brian.

'I mean apart from that,' said Dougal.

'I don't know,' said Brian. 'I saw him and got a bit frightened, so I came to ask your advice and counsel.'

'Very wise,' said Dougal, 'but what do you want me to do about it?'

'Well, I thought you'd go out there and catch him and ask him what he's doing and tell him anything he says will be used in evidence and all that sort of thing,' said Brian. 'Got a spare cup?'

'Get it yourself,' said Dougal, 'you're not helpless.'

Brian helped himself to tea.

'Well, are you going?' he asked.

'Give me time,' said Dougal, 'these things shouldn't be rushed into. Is he armed?'

'Yes, two,' said Brian, 'like most people.'

Dougal controlled himself with difficulty.

'I mean, does he have a gun or anything, you great clump!' he said.

'Well, I don't know about a gun, but he had something pretty wicked-looking in his hands,' said Brian. 'It frightened me.'

'Anything frightens you,' said Dougal. 'Come on.'

'I've not finished my tea,' said Brian, quickly.

'No time for that,' said Dougal, who had finished his. 'Come on!'

So they set out to investigate the prowler.

Outside it was very dark.

'Dark, isn't it?' said Brian, loudly.

Dougal leapt behind a tree.

'Sorry,' said Brian. 'Did I make you jump?'

Dougal came out.

'If you say another word I'm leaving,' he said.

'Sorry,' said Brian.

They went on.

'Where did you see this prowler?' said Dougal.

Brian didn't answer.

'I said where did you see him?' said Dougal.

Brian still didn't answer.

'What's the matter with you?' said Dougal. 'Gone deaf?'

'You told me not to speak, old captain,' said Brian.

'Really,' said Dougal, 'you're as thick as two short planks. I just meant don't speak until you're spoken to.'

'Oh, I see,' said Brian. 'Over there.'

'What?' said Dougal.

'I saw him over there,' said Brian.

They looked over there and there was the prowler, definitely prowling.

They hid behind a bush and watched. The prowler was dressed in black from head to foot and behaving in a very strange way.

He was going up to each flower in the garden and squirting it with a big brass garden spray. He didn't miss a single flower and every now and then he refilled his spray from some bottles he had in a bag.

'What a funny carry-on,' said Brian.

'You can say that again,' said Dougal.

'What a funny carry-on,' said Brian.

'Oh, be quiet,' said Dougal.

They went a little nearer.

'Shall we pounce?' said Brian. 'I'm a very good pouncer.'

'By the time you'd pounced he'd be three miles away,' said Dougal. 'You can't even run let alone pounce.'

'Well, you pounce then,' said Brian.

'And get squirted?' said Dougal. 'It might be poison in that squirter.'

'Why would he want to poison the flowers?' said Brian.

'I can't think,' said Dougal. 'Perhaps he's dotty.'

'Oh dear,' moaned Brian, 'alone with a mad squirter.'

'You're not alone,' said Dougal, icily. 'I'm here.'

'Oh, yes,' said Brian.

The dark figure moved away. They followed. It went to some rose-bushes and started squirting again.

'At this rate there won't be a flower left,' said Dougal. 'We must act.'

'Do you think we should get Florence?' said Brian.

Dougal looked at him pityingly.

'Rouse a young lady in the middle of the night?' he said. 'What a cowardly suggestion. Are you a man or a mouse?'

Brian thought.

'I'm a snail,' he said.

Busy talking, neither Dougal nor Brian noticed the dark figure with his spray had circled round and was coming straight towards them. He was quite close when they saw him.

'Freeze!' hissed Dougal, and they froze.

The figure came very close, stopped, put down his bag

and peered at them.

'Funny looking flowers,' he muttered, squirting Dougal and Brian with his spray, and moving on.

Dougal and Brian didn't twitch.

'Squirted, by George!' said Dougal.

'Oh, was it George?' said Brian.

Dougal sniffed.

There was a very strong smell of roses everywhere.

'Have you been using scent?' he asked.

'Certainly not!' said Brian.

'Then what's that smell?' said Dougal.

'I think it's you,' said Brian.

'Choose your words, snail,' said Dougal, 'and come on.'

So, smelling like two rose-bushes, they followed the man with the spray. He was travelling quite fast and seemed to have finished spraying the flowers.

'Where's he going?' panted Dougal.

'Perhaps he's run out of squirt and is going to get some more,' said Brian.

Sure enough, the man stopped at a house and went in. Brian and Dougal stopped too.

'Hey, old fellow sleuth!' said Brian, 'that's Mr MacHenry's house.'

'Odder and odder,' said Dougal. 'What's he doing in Mr MacHenry's house?'

'Perhaps he's going to squirt him,' said Brian.

'Why would he want to squirt Mr MacHenry?' said Dougal.

'Well, he squirted us,' said Brian.

'True,' said Dougal, thoughtfully.

They went nearer and looked in the window. Inside it was all dark and sinister.

'I hope Mr MacHenry's all right,' said Brian. 'I like him.'

'I'm sure he'll be very pleased to hear it,' said Dougal, 'if we ever see him again.'

'Oh, don't say that!' said

Brian. 'I like him.'

Suddenly all the lights went on in Mr MacHenry's house and they saw . . . Mr MacHenry.

'He's safe! He's safe!' whispered Brian.

'But what's he doing?' whispered Dougal.

They watched. Mr MacHenry moved about the room busily. He picked up several coloured bottles and put them in a row. Then he took a big coloured jug and started to fill them. On the table was the large spray.

Dougal looked at Brian and Brian looked at Dougal.

'The phantom squirter!' whispered Dougal.

'Old MacHenry!' whispered Brian.

'Whoever would have thought it?' said Dougal.

'I would,' said Brian.

'I never liked him.'

'I wish you'd make up your mind,' said Dougal.

They watched again.

Mr MacHenry finished filling the bottles and packed them into a large bag. He picked up the spray and went to the door.

'He's going to start again!' squeaked Brian.

The light went out and they heard the door open.

'We'll follow and observe,' said Dougal.

'After you,' said Brian.

'You're a coward,' said Dougal.

'I know,' said Brian.

They followed Mr MacHenry. Every now and then he would stop, squirt a few flowers and go on. Dougal and Brian were in a bit of a quandary. What should they do? Ask Mr MacHenry to explain? Report him to the police? Tell him to stop? It was a problem.

'I'm exhausted,' said Brian. 'Give us a ride.'

'Oh, get on then,' said Dougal, and Brian climbed on to Dougal's head.

'Not on my head!' said Dougal. 'Great oaf!'

'Sorry,' said Brian.

They went on. Mr MacHenry stoppd at a little gate in

a high wall, opened it and went in.

'We've got him!' said Dougal. 'Come on!' And before Brian could object he shot through the gate and slammed it shut behind them.

'Er . . . you realise what you've done, old thing?' said Brian.

'Yes, we've trapped him!' said Dougal.

'You've trapped us too,' said Brian. 'We are alone behind this high wall with the mad squirter.'

Dougal blenched.

'Back!' he screeched, but it was too late. Mr MacHenry had heard them and was approaching.

'Keep back, fiend!' said Dougal.

'Yes, keep back, fiend!' said Brian, from behind Dougal.

'Fiend?' said Mr MacHenry, coming up to them with his spray. 'What do you mean, "FIEND"?'

'You've been killing all the flowers,' squeaked Brian. 'You are a flowercidal maniac!'

'Exactly!' said Dougal.

Mr MacHenry laughed.

'It's no laughing matter!' they said.

But Mr MacHenry laughed again.

'I'm afraid you've got it all wrong,' he said. 'I'm not killing any flowers.'

'Then what are you doing?' they demanded.

'Well, it's a secret,' said Mr MacHenry, 'but if you promise not to tell anyone I'll tell you.'

And he explained that in the garden, which was a bit magic, the flowers lasted for ever but the *scent* of the flowers tended to wear off, so he had to go round every now and then putting the scent back with his special spray.

Brian and Dougal looked at him.

'Why do you do it in the middle of the night?' they asked.

'Well, I don't want anyone to know,' said Mr MacHenry. 'It's a secret, you see?'

Brian and Dougal promised not to tell.

'Well, I think you'd better come back to my place for breakfast,' said Mr MacHenry. 'You must be hungry.'

'Just one thing,' said Dougal, 'what's this place here behind this big wall?'

'Oh, this is where I grow the special flowers which give me the scent for the other flowers,' said Mr MacHenry. 'And that's a secret too.'

'Well, I shouldn't worry,' said Dougal. 'It's all so complicated I've forgotten already.'

'Come on then,' said Mr MacHenry, 'and I'll make you one of my special breakfasts. Toast and honey, waffles and treacle, scones and jam, carrot salad, and a cup of tea.'

They went.

'I've always liked him,' whispered Brian.

# The Tea Party

Dougal was at home early one morning sipping a cup of tea and thinking about LIFE. He finished his tea and thought LIFE was perhaps a little tedious. He poured himself another cup and sipped. He brightened.

'Oh, I don't know, perhaps it's not too bad.'

He put down his empty cup.

'Then again,' he thought, 'perhaps it *is*. Maybe it's something to do with it being *Tuesday*. I'm not at my best on a *Tuesday*. Tuesdays seldom have potential, I find.'

There was a knock at the door.

Dougal got up.

Another knock, louder.

'All right, all right, I'm coming,' said Dougal.

A third knock, even louder.

Dougal opened the door.

It was Brian wearing a very large blue cap and carrying a very large canvas bag.

'Lovely morning, sir,' he said, brightly.

'And what have you come as?' said Dougal.

'What do you mean?' said Brian.

'I mean,' said Dougal, mildly, 'that you are obviously masquerading as something. I just wondered what it was, that's all.'

'You're being very mild,' said Brian, suspiciously. 'Can I come in?'

'I can't think of any reason why you should,' said Dougal.

'Postmen are always asked in,' said Brian, 'and I'm a postman. I bring greetings from afar through hail, snow sun and mud and I demand to be asked in and provided with comforts.'

'What had you in mind?' said Dougal.

'Well, isn't the kettle on?' said Brian. 'Postmen always get a cup of tea when they've got a letter for someone.'

He pushed past Dougal, went in, sat down and started to whistle a little tune.

Dougal put the kettle on.

'Boiling already?' said Brian.

'Of course not,' said Dougal.

'Oh, I thought I heard it whistling,' said Brian.

'That was *you*,' said Dougal.

'Oh,' said Brian.

Dougal made some tea, gave a cup to Brian and sat down.

'Lovely day,' said Brian.

'You've mentioned that,' said Dougal.

'Oh,' said Brian.

He finished his tea.

'Well, I must be off,' he said, getting up.

'Haven't you forgotten something?' said Dougal.

Brian paused.

'No, I don't think so, old chum.'

'Sure?' said Dougal.

'Positive,' said Brian. 'Goodbye.'

He went towards the door.

Dougal stepped on the canvas bag as Brian went by, and Brian somersaulted and landed on his shell upside down, rocking gently.

'You tripped me up,' he squeaked, accusingly.

'An accident,' said Dougal.

'Sure?' said Brian.

'Positive,' said Dougal.

'Oh, that's all right then,' said Brian, rocking.

'Lucky though,' mused Dougal, 'or you might have gone without giving me my letter.'

'Good heavens, so I might,' said Brian, and he tried to right himself.

'Having trouble?' said Dougal, rummaging in Brian's canvas bag.

'Hey!' squeaked Brian. 'You're not allowed to do that. Those letters are the property of Her Majesty's Post Office.'

He gave a great heave, righted himself and scuttled into the bag.

'Desist rummaging,' he said, popping his head out.

Dougal pulled at the strap on the bag and lifted it up. Brian disappeared with a thump inside.

'I shall count three,' said Dougal, 'and then if my letter doesn't appear I shall hang this bag on a hook and go on holiday.'

'We postmen aren't easily frightened,' shouted Brian from inside the bag.

'One . . .' said Dougal. 'Two.'

A letter appeared. Dougal dropped the bag.

Brian crawled out.

'I may resign, he said, slowly.

'Someone, somewhere, needs a letter from you,' said Dougal. 'There's the door – goodbye.'

'I'll report you to the Minister of Posts and Telecommunications,' said Brian.

'Do,' said Dougal.

'He's very fierce,' said Brian.

'Oh, is he?' said Dougal.

Brian went to the door.

'It's an invitation,' he said. 'We've all got one,' and he went out very quickly.

Dougal rushed after him.

'Rotter!' he shouted. 'Spoilsport!'

He jumped up and down with fury.

'Oooh! I hate knowing what's in a letter before I open it. Takes all the fun away. I hope your cap shrinks!' he shouted at Brian.

'See you later!' Brian shouted back.

Dougal sat down to read his letter. It was an invitation from Florence. She'd asked everyone to tea that day and said he was to be sure to come as she's got everything arranged and lots of lovely things in. 'Just come as you are,' the letter finished.

'Well, I'm not likely to go as anyone else,' giggled

Dougal, fiddling around in his drawer for a clean collar.

He brushed his hair and then had a sudden thought.

'I must take her something – a present – some flowers perhaps.'

He hummed a little tune.

'There'll be *cakes*,' he thought, 'so I'll take a lot of flowers.'

Outside the sun was shining and it was very hot. There didn't seem to be many flowers about.

'Someone's been at them,' thought Dougal, darkly. 'I shall go to Mr MacHenry's. He'll have some in his greenhouse.'

But Mr MacHenry hadn't.

'It's this dry weather we've been having,' he said. 'The flowers have withered. We need rain.'

'And, I need flowers,' said Dougal. 'Haven't you even got a petunia?'

'Not one,' said Mr MacHenry. 'Need rain, you see, and we won't have rain while the wind is in the South.'

'While the *what* is *where*?' said Dougal.

Mr MacHenry pointed to the weathercock on top of the church.

'See that? he said. 'Been like that for weeks. Wind's in the South. Needs to be in the West for rain.'

'Oh,' said Dougal, thoughtfully, 'thank you. Er . . . West, you say?'

'West,' said Mr MacHenry, and he went into his greenhouse and started mulching a few things.

Dougal went slowly towards the church. He had to have flowers for Florence – he always took flowers when he went to tea. There seemed to be only one thing to be done. So he did it . . .

Halfway up the church steeple he stopped for breath and looked down.

Everything below seemed very small. He saw Florence's house in the distance, and the Roundabout by Mr Rusty's house was just a speck of colour.

'I hope I'm doing the right thing,' he thought, panting on up.

He passed two pigeons sitting on a ledge.

'Afternoon,' he said.

The pigeons remained silent.

'Suit yourselves,' grunted Dougal, clambering on.

'Was that a dog?' said one of the pigeons.

'Don't be silly, Phyllis,' murmured the other.

Dougal reached the top and paused to get his breath.

He looked at the weathercock. The weathercock looked back at him. It was a tense moment.

'Er . . . I have a request,' said Dougal. 'We need a little rain and you're pointing the wrong way. Might I trouble you to turn to the West?'

'Got any authority?' said the weathercock. 'Letter from the Ministry? Chitty from the Met. Office?'

'Not exactly . . .' began Dougal.

'Can't be done then,' said the weathercock. 'Not without a chitty. In triplicate,' he added.

'I haven't got time to get a chitty,' said Dougal. 'I'm in a hurry.'

'Oh yes, they all say that,' said the weathercock. 'But I don't move a point without a chitty.'

Dougal sighed, eased himself up a little, and slipped.

'Whoops!' he shouted, grabbing the weathercock and

spinning around.

'Stop that!' said the weathercock, sharply.

'I can't, said Dougal, rotating.

'I'm getting dizzy,' shouted the weathercock.

'You're not the only one,' screeched Dougal.

A wind started to blow. The weathercock went round faster and faster.

'You haven't got a chitty!' shouted the weathercock.

'Oh, shut up!' shouted Dougal, trying to find a footing somewhere.

The weathercock bent a little. The wind blew more and more. It started to thunder.

'Oh, I hate it – I hate it!' moaned Dougal.

The weathercock bent a little more. The storm got more and more furious.

Another bend and a squeak, and the weathercock jammed and stopped.

Dougal was thrown off and found himself slithering down the steeple with thunder and lightning crashing all around him. He passed the pigeons very fast.

'I've seen that dog again,' said one.

'I'm getting very worried about you, Phyllis,' said the other.

Dougal reached the bottom just as it started to pour with rain. The weathercock was pointing firmly to the West and Dougal was soaked to the skin.

'Now see what you've done!' shouted the weathercock. 'I'm all bent!'

'I'll let you have a chitty later,' shouted Dougal. And he giggled.

There was a peal of thunder and the rain teemed down. With water dripping off him, Dougal hurried to

Mr MacHenry's.

'Lovely weather!' he shouted, through the crashing thunder. Mr MacHenry didn't answer. He was busy trying to keep the rain out of his greenhouse with a mop.

'Flowers growing?' shouted Dougal.

There was another crash and a wave of water carried Dougal and Mr MacHenry right into the greenhouse.

'The stream's overflowed!' shouted Mr MacHenry, as they sloshed around amongst the flowerpots. 'Everything's ruined!'

They climbed up on to a shelf as the water rose higher.

'Er . . . I thought you needed rain?' said Dougal.

'Rain I needed,' said Mr MacHenry. 'Floods I can do without.'

He grabbed a passing pot of geraniums.

'Look at that! Pitifully bedraggled!'

'Can I have it?' said Dougal.

'Well, I don't want it,' said Mr MacHenry.

Dougal took the pot and looked down. The water seemed very deep and muddy.

'You don't have a boat handy, do you?' he asked.

Mr MacHenry finally snapped.

'No, I do not! This is a nursery, not Portsmouth harbour. Oh dear, oh dear! It'll take me weeks to get this lot right again.'

Dougal decided it was time to leave. He put the pot of geraniums on his head, launched himself into the water and started to swim towards Florence's house.

He met a flock of ducks.

'Lovely weather!' they quacked.

'All right for some!' panted Dougal, battling against the current.

'Did you know you've got a plant pot on your head?' they asked.

'Yes,' gritted Dougal.

He arrived at Florence's. Everyone was there looking out the window, Mr Rusty, Brian, Ermintrude, Dylan and Zebedee.

'Let me in!' shouted Dougal.

'We can't, the water will come in too!' they shouted back.

'Then open the window!' screeched Dougal.

Florence opened the window and Dougal heaved himself up and fell inside on to the carpet.

'I say, you're a bit squelchy,' said Brian.

'You'd be squelchy if you'd been through what I've been through,' said Dougal.

He turned to Florence.

'I've brought you a flower,' he said.

'Oh, Dougal, how lovely,' said Florence. 'You shouldn't have bothered.'

'Oh, it was no bother,' said Dougal. 'Any cake left?'

And there was.

# The Roundabout

The next day they discovered a terrible thing. The great storm had damaged the Magic Roundabout and Mr Rusty was very upset. He'd gone to start it up as usual and had found it all bent and twisted.

'Must have been struck by lightning,' he said, mournfully. 'I don't like to worry, as you know, but it's a catastrophe . . . a catastrophe.'

They all walked round looking at the Roundabout. It was certainly very out of shape.

'Isn't it *awful*, Dougal,' said Florence.

Dougal gulped, feeling very responsible when he remembered the weathercock.

'Awful,' he squeaked, 'awful.'

'We must do something about it,' said Florence, firmly.

Everyone agreed that something must be done about it and they all sat down to think what to do.

'I know!' said Brian. 'I know! It's simple! It's so simple I don't know why we didn't think of it straight away.'

'Tell us, Brian,' they said.

'Yes, come on, master mind,' said Dougal.

'The Roundabout is broken – true?' said Brian.

'True,' they all said.

'Then we must mend it,' said Brian. 'Simple!'

He looked round triumphantly.

'How about a round of applause?' he said.

'How about a thump on the bonce?' said Dougal.

'Dougal!' said Florence. 'Don't be vulgar,' and she explained to Brian that mending the Roundabout had occurred to all of them; they were just thinking about the best way to do it.

'Oh, sorry,' said Brian. 'I thought perhaps the fundamentals of the problem had been overlooked.'

'Our fundamental problem is *you*,' said Dougal. 'Now be quiet and think.'

They all thought again.

'I've got it!' said Brian. 'This time I've really got it!'

'If you haven't you're going to have *something*,' said Dougal, darkly.

'No, listen,' said Brian. 'We need to mend the Roundabout – true?'

'True,' they all said.

'So why don't we ring up the Roundabout menders?' said Brian. 'Simple.'

They all thought.

'That's a great idea, man,' said Dylan, and he dropped off to sleep with relief.

'Well, I must say it does *seem* to be a good idea, small creature,' said Ermintrude.

'It's a *possibility*,' said Mr Rusty, thoughtfully.

'Yes, a possibility,' said Florence.

Dougal got up and went over to Brian.

'Snail,' he said, 'you have a great talent.'

'Thank you,' said Brian, proudly.

'There are just one or two minor points I should like to raise,' said Dougal.

'Raise them,' said Brian, confidently.

'One,' said Dougal, 'we don't know any Roundabout menders to ring up.

'Two – I doubt if anyone knows any Roundabout menders to ring up.

'Three – I doubt if there *are* any Roundabout menders who could be rung up.

'Four, we haven't got a telephone book and five, WE HAVEN'T GOT A TELEPHONE!!!!'

'Steady, Dougal,' murmured Florence.

'Well!' said Dougal. 'It's always the same. Roundabout menders, indeed!! Really!! Now let's all think sensibly about what to do. You too!!' he said to Brian.

But Brian had gone.

'Where's he gone?' said Dougal.

'He said he wouldn't be a minute,' said Mr Rusty.

'Well, at least we can think in peace,' said Dougal.

And they all thought again.

There was a rumble in the distance.

'Not another thunderstorm, I hope,' said Mr Rusty, nervously.

'I think it's the train, dear heart,' said Ermintrude.

But it wasn't, it was a lorry.

It got nearer and nearer.

It was a very old lorry and it made a lot of noise. It came to a halt by the Roundabout, steam sizzling out of the radiator and the engine making all sorts of suspicious noises. Painted on the side was:

NETTLESHIP & BUTT
ROUNDABOUT MENDING & DENTURE
REPAIRS
HURDY GURDY SPECIALISTS
ESTIMATES FREE!

'I don't believe it,' squeaked Dougal.

'What a coincidence,' said Florence.

But it wasn't a coincidence because Brian got out of the lorry.

'Friends of mine,' he said. 'Not a lot of work on at the moment – able to come at once to our assistance. May I introduce Mr Nettleship and Mr Butt.'

Two very old men got out of the lorry.

One was very tall and the other was very short, and they were both dressed in long overalls and big boots.

'Roundabout menders,' said Brian, looking at Dougal.

Dougal sighed.

'You can't win, can you? he said to Florence.

'Cheer up, Dougal,' said Florence.

Mr Rusty explained the problem to the Roundabout

menders and Mr Nettleship and Mr Butt walked round looking at the damage.

'1913 model?' said Mr Nettleship.

'More like 1915, I'd say,' said Mr Butt.

'With respect, Gasgoigne,' said Mr Nettleship, 'I think you're wrong.'

'And with respect, Ron,' said Mr Butt, 'I think I'm right.'

'Er . . . it's a 1914 model,' said Mr Rusty.

'Ah!' said Mr Nettleship and Mr Butt. 'Ah!'

'Then it's got self-winding elastic sprockets,' said Mr Butt.

'And apple-wood connections to the rollers,' said Mr Nettleship.

'Ah!' they both said again.

Dougal and Brian giggled like anything.

'I wonder if it's got fur-lined quonkers?' said Brian.

'Or gronge-grabbers on the waffles?' said Dougal.

And they both fell about laughing like anything.

'Quiet, you two!' said Florence, sharply.

'Sorry,' they said, giggling.

Everyone sat down to watch the experts at work.

Mr Nettleship and Mr Butt walked over to their lorry and pulled out two big bags of tools.

'I think the first problem is to stabilise the equilibrium joints,' said Mr Nettleship.

'Indubitably,' said Mr Butt.

'We shall need a little assistance,' they said.

Everyone was very ready to help.

'Now to get at the equilibrium joints we need the Roundabout on its side,' said Mr Butt. 'This means attaching a rope to the top, giving a hearty pull and putting a wedge underneath.'

So they attached a rope to the top and gave a hearty pull.

The Roundabout fell over.

'Was that a bit too hearty?' said Brian.

'Get it off me!' screeched Dougal.

'Oh dear, Dougal,' said Florence, 'are you all right?'

'I'm as all right as anyone could be with a roundabout on top of him,' huffed Dougal.

Mr Nettleship and Mr Butt came round to look.

'If you could stay there for a little while,' they said to Dougal, 'it will greatly assist us. We have the machine at just the right angle. You are, if anything, better than a wedge.'

'I'm so glad,' said Dougal.

'It's nice to be useful, isn't it?' said Brian, brightly.

'Go away,' said Dougal.

The Roundabout menders got to work. All sorts of tools came out of the tool bags and there was a lot of banging and crashing and wrenching.

'May I trouble you for the pinchers, Ron?' said Mr Butt.

'Certainly, Gasgoigne,' said Mr Nettleship, passing them.

The work went on and the Roundabout gradually took shape again. A final twist and the last bend was straightened.

'There, then,' said Mr Butt.

'Perfect,' said Mr Nettleship.

'Er . . . finished?' said Mr Rusty.

They said they were. All that was needed was to put the Roundabout the right way up and test for stability and accuracy. Another good pull on the rope was needed.

Everyone got hold of the rope and pulled. The Roundabout straightened up with a jerk, and Dougal flipped straight up into the air and landed quivering on the top.

'Get me down!' he shrieked.

But before anyone could stop them Mr Nettleship and Mr Butt were testing the Roundabout for stability and accuracy. They made it go very fast and then they made it go very slow and then they made it go very fast again. Finally they stopped it.

'It's all right now,' they said, 'except for one small thing.'

'What's that?' said Mr Rusty.

'That mascot on the top is too heavy in our opinion. It spoils the accuracy of the plonk-bearings. It should be replaced – perhaps by a small flag.'

'I'm not a mascot,' screamed Dougal. 'I'm here by accident!! And I feel very sick!!'

'You look lovely,' shouted Brian.

'I'm not interested in your opinion,' shouted Dougal. 'Get a ladder!!'

They got a ladder and Dougal was helped down. He sat on the ground quivering.

'Now I don't wish to complain,' he said.

'You know me, no one could be less complaining. But I have been used as a wedge. I have been used as a test for stability and equilibrium – would it be too much to ask if anyone is thinking of making a cup of tea?'

'I could do you a lettuce butty,' said Brian, brightly.

But Florence realised Dougal's needs and everyone went into Mr Rusty's place for tea. Mr Nettleship and Mr Butt had a cup each and then said they had to go.

'Got a big job on in Stockport,' they said.

Everyone waved goodbye as the lorry rattled away.

'Er . . . anyone feel like a ride on the Roundabout?' said Mr Rusty.

'I think I'll just have another cup of tea and watch,' said Dougal.

Which he did.

# The Magic Book

Everyone had been invited to Zebedee's house to watch him do some magic tricks. He entertained them for a long time. He made balloons appear and disappear. He put big boxes into small boxes. He cut paper into pieces and made it whole again. Finally, he produced a pigeon out of a bowler hat and an egg out of Dougal's ear. It was all highly enjoyable.

'Would anyone else like to have a go?' he asked.

Brian said he would be very interested to have a go. Dougal sniggered.

'That snail couldn't produce water out of a tap,' he whispered.

'Hush, Dougal,' said Florence.

Brian stood on a stool beside Zebedee.

'For my first trick,' he said in a high-pitched voice. 'I shall produce a rabbit out of this very small paper-bag which once contained treacle toffee. The rabbit is called Fred and he's very nervous, so I shall have to ask for complete silence.'

There was a squeak of laughter from Dougal.

'*Complete* silence,' said Brian, fiercely.

'Sorry, Houdini,' said Dougal, giggling.

'Now hush, Dougal,' said Florence.

The others told Dougal to hush as well because they all wanted Brian to go on with his trick.

'I shall go on with my trick,' said Brian, 'and produce this rabbit called Fred out of this small paper-bag.'

'What's the paper-bag called?' shouted Dougal, laughing like anything.

Everyone shushed Dougal again and Zebedee said if he promised to be quiet he could have a go later.

'Sorry all,' said Dougal. 'On, mollusc.'

Brian coughed.

'Er . . . thank you. Rabbit out of paper-bag trick coming up.'

He picked up the paper-bag, gave it a little tap with a wand and said:

'Fred – appear!'

Nothing happened. Brian peered into the bag.

'Try again, dear thing,' said Ermintrude.

Brian tried again. He tapped the paper-bag and said louder:

'Fred – appear!!'

Again nothing happened.

'Go inside and get him!' hooted Dougal.

'Fred – appear!!!' shouted Brian, desperately.

No one noticed Zebedee's moustache give a little twitch, and suddenly the very small paper-bag burst open and a large white rabbit appeared.

'Gracious!' said Mr Rusty.

'Goodness!' said Florence.

'I don't believe it,' shouted Dougal. 'I do not believe it! IT WAS UP YOUR SLEEVE!'

'I HAVEN'T GOT ANY SLEEVES!' shouted Brian.

'THEN IT WAS IN YOUR HAT!' shouted Dougal.

'I'VE STILL GOT MY HAT ON!' screeched Brian.
'Please! Please!' said Florence. 'Don't shout!'

And everyone applauded Brian's marvellous trick
while Dougal grumbled away to himself.

The white rabbit called Fred came to the edge of the
table and peered.

'Dylan, baby!' he called.

Dylan woke up with a start.

'Er . . . what!? . . . like . . . what?' he said.

'It's me – Fred!' said Fred. 'How have you been?'

'Well, friend Fred!' said Dylan. 'It's been a long time. Still doing the paper-bag act?'

'Still doing it,' said Fred, happily. 'Still playing guitar?'

'Still playing, man,' said Dylan. 'How's Elsie?'

'Great, Dyl baby, great,' said Fred.

'WHO'S ELSIE!?' shrieked Dougal.

Dylan and Fred wandered off talking together while everyone else discussed how the trick could possibly have been done. Brian sat down next to Dougal.

'Good trick, eh?' he said.

Dougal glowered.

'I refuse to speak to you,' he said.

'Why, old matey?' said Brian.

'Because for one thing,' said Dougal, 'I thought that trick was very showy and vulgar, and for another thing – what happened to all that treacle toffee?'

'I ate it,' said Brian, happily.

'Typical!' said Dougal. 'I share my last cup of tea with you, but I don't get a sniff of any treacle toffee when it's going.'

'But it was a good rabbit trick though, wasn't it?' said Brian.

'Oh, be quiet,' said Dougal.

Zebedee tapped with his wand.

'Anyone else like to have a go?' he asked.

Florence said she would be interested to try and everyone applauded.

'I shall attempt a very little trick,' said Florence, modestly. 'I shall try to make someone disappear. For this I shall need a volunteer from the audience.'

There was no great rush to volunteer.

'May I have a volunteer, please?' said Florence.

'This snail's volunteering,' shouted Dougal, pushing Brian.

'No, I'm not,' said Brian. 'I've done my bit. *You* volunteer.'

'Not likely,' said Dougal. 'I was told never to trust ladies with wands.'

'Oh, it's quite safe,' said Florence.

'Well, in that case,' said Ermintrude bravely, 'I shall volunteer.'

Everyone burst out laughing, but Ermintrude stepped on to the stage and looked round.

'I'm just as capable of disappearing as anyone else,' she said severely. 'There's no call for ribaldry.'

She turned to Florence.

'Ready, dear?' she said.

Florence looked a little apprehensively at Zebedee, but Zebedee gave her a little wink of reassurance.

'Go ahead,' he said.

Florence waved the wand nervously. Nothing happened.

'Shouldn't you put me in a box or something, dear heart?' said Ermintrude.

'I haven't got a box!' said Florence.

'Use the table-cloth!' shouted Dougal, helpless with laughter.

'Or a match-box,' shouted Brian, wheezing and giggling.

Ermintrude told Dougal and Brian to be quiet.

'*Try* the table-cloth,' she said to Florence.

Florence threw the table-cloth over Ermintrude. It didn't cover her completely – her legs and tail still showed.

'She's still there!' shrieked Brian and Dougal, laughing.

'I haven't started yet,' said Florence.

'Oh, sorry,' they said, tittering.

Florence walked slowly round Ermintrude tapping her with the wand.

'Ermintrude, disappear!' she said.

Zebedee's moustache gave another little twitch and suddenly Ermintrude's legs disappeared leaving the table-cloth with Ermintrude inside it apparently suspended in mid-air.

'Have I gone, dear?' said Ermintrude.

'Not exactly,' said Florence.

Dougal and Brian were finding it difficult to contain themselves.

'No visible means of support!' they shrieked, holding on to each other and crying with laughter.

Florence tapped again. This time Ermintrude's legs reappeared and her body disappeared, leaving the table-cloth just like a table with four legs and a tail.

Everyone roared with laughter.

'What time's tea?' hooted Dougal.

'I ain't got no body!' screamed Brian and they both laughed so much they ended up in a heap on the floor.

'What's happening now, dear?' said Ermintrude.

'I'm not sure,' said Florence, desperately.

She gave a further tap just as Zebedee's moustache gave another twitch, and this time the table-cloth floated to the ground and Ermintrude, with a faint 'moo', was gone completely.

Everyone gathered round. Mr Rusty lifted up the table-cloth. Ermintrude certainly wasn't there.

'What a marvellous trick,' said Mr Rusty.

'Marvellous,' said Mr MacHenry.

Dougal looked at Brian and Brian looked at Dougal.

'All right then,' they said. 'BRING HER BACK!!'

Florence laughed and so did Zebedee, and then Dougal realised *Zebedee* had done the trick and Zebedee had done the rabbit trick too.

'It was *you*,' he said to Zebedee, 'wasn't it?'

'Anything's possible,' said Zebedee.

There was a YOO! HOO! from the other room.

Ermintrude put her head round the door.

'The kettle's on,' she said. 'Anyone for tea?'

Everyone was very glad to see Ermintrude back and also quite glad that tea was ready.

'Coming for a cup, old chumpy chops?' said Brian.

'Yes . . . er . . . in just a minute,' said Dougal. 'You go on and . . . er . . . keep me a cake.'

Everyone went into the other room for tea and Dougal heard them asking Ermintrude what it was like to disappear, etc. . . . etc. . . .

He tiptoed across and closed the door.

'Now,' he thought, 'let's have a bit of magic. I wonder where he keeps it.'

He rummaged around the drawers of Zebedee's desk and finally came across a little book labelled:

O.H.M.S.

DANGER – MAGIC SPELLS (MARK II)

'Aha!' thought Dougal. 'Oho!' And he looked through the book. There were various chapters headed

'Things out of paper-bags'

'Things disappearing'

'Things reappearing'

'Things exploding'

but right at the end there was a short chapter which just said,

'SECRET THINGS – NOT TO BE READ BY ANYONE'.

'Oho!' thought Dougal. 'Aha!' And he started to read.

Next door everyone was enjoying tea and cakes. Dylan and Fred had come back and Ermintrude was telling them all about her disappearing act with Florence.

'It was such fun,' she said. 'Just like floating.'

'We know the feeling,' said Dylan and Fred.

Florence took another cake.

'Where's Dougal?' she said.

No one knew. It was unlike Dougal to be missing when it was tea-time.

'He said he wouldn't be a minute,' said Brian.

Zebedee looked thoughtful.

'Did he stay in *there*?' he asked.

'Yes,' said Brian.

'Oh dear,' said Zebedee.

There was a bang from the other room, then another bang and a crash. The door blew open and purple smoke billowed out.

'Oh dear,' said Zebedee again.

Everyone rushed into the other room. The smoke was very dense.

'Open a window,' shouted Mr MacHenry.

Mr Rusty opened a window, and everyone waved their hankies and flapped and blew to make the smoke disappear. When it was all gone they looked around. The room was empty. On the table was a book and on the floor Zebedee's magic wand. There was no sign of Dougal.

'Whatever can have happened?' said Florence.

They all wandered about looking for a sign of Dougal, but there was nothing.

'Listen!' said Brian.

Everyone listened.

'STOP TRAMPLING ABOUT!!' said the voice again.

'I know that voice,' said Brian, ' – it's old shaggy! Come out, hidden friend!!'

'I AM OUT!' said the voice. 'I'M DOWN HERE!!'

Everyone looked. Under the table was a very, very small furry bundle. It was Dougal, about two inches long and looking very sad.

Brian went very close and looked at him.

'My little friend!' he said. 'Why are you so small?'

'I'VE NOT BEEN WELL,' said Dougal sarcastically.

'Just a minute,' said Brian, 'you're not very easy to hear. Stay there!'

He got a piece of cardboard and told Florence to twist it into a trumpet shape. Then he put it close to Dougal.

'Speak now, old chum,' he said.

'DO SOMETHING!' said Dougal, so loudly that Brian fell over backwards.

'What *happened*, Dougal?' said Florence.

'I think I know what happened,' said Zebedee, sternly. 'You've been reading my book, haven't you?'

Dougal nodded miserably.

'YES!!' he bellowed through the trumpet. 'I'M SORRY!!'

'So you should be,' said Zebedee, and he winked at Florence.

'HOW LONG WILL I BE LIKE THIS?!!' asked Dougal.

'There's no need to shout, wee one,' said Ermintrude.

'Can you turn him back?' whispered Florence to Zebedee.

'Yes,' whispered Zebedee.

'Are you sorry?' he asked Dougal.

'YES!' said Dougal.

'Will you ever do it again?' asked Zebedee.

'NEVER!' said Dougal.

'Hey, you're not going to make him big again, are you?' said Brian. 'I like him like that.'

'DON'T INTERFERE!' shouted Dougal.

'But you're lovely little,' said Brian.

'You are rather,' said Florence.

'Adorable,' said Ermintrude.

'ROTTERS!' shouted Dougal, and he scuttled on to Brian, up his shell and on to his head. 'ROTTERS!'

Zebedee muttered a few words and gave a twitch of his moustache.

Dougal was suddenly his normal size again and Brian collapsed with a 'WHOOSH'.

Dougal shook himself, looked at Brian and giggled.
'Who's your flat friend?' he said to Florence.
'Dougal, you're *awful*,' said Florence.
'I know,' said Dougal. 'Any cake left?'
And of course, there was.

# PART 2

# *Dougal's Scottish holiday*

# *It is decided*

One morning, Dougal woke up very slowly. First he opened one eye – then he opened the other; then he closed the first eye and tried using just one; then he closed the second eye and started all over again by opening both very wide and very suddenly.

It was a terrible shock, so he closed them and went back to sleep.

*Come into the garden, Maud,*
*For the black bat night has flown . . .*

sang a voice, very loudly and not very tunefully. It was Brian.

*Come into the garden, Fred,*
*For the black bat night has fled . . .*

he sang, louder than ever and very close to Dougal's ear. Dougal sat up with a start.

'What!' he screeched. 'What! What! What!'

*Come into the garden, Ron,*
*For the black bat night has gone!*

sang Brian, going over to the stove and putting the kettle on.

Dougal watched him from the bed coldly.

'Have you gone out of your mind completely?' he said.

'Good morning, good morning, good morning!' shouted Brian.

Dougal got out of bed and went very close to Brian.

'You've come very close to me,' said Brian, nervously.

Dougal looked at him *very* hard and then spoke *very* slowly and *very* quietly.

'Mollusc,' he said, 'listen carefully. In the first place you have woken me up. In the second place you are making a great deal of noise. In the third place it's the middle of the night and in the fourth place what are you doing in my place?' He paused.

'Take your time and answer slowly,' he said.

'I get the feeling you're displeased with me,' said Brian, cheerfully. 'Am I right?'

Dougal made some tea.

'Just answer the question,' he said.

'Ah!' said Brian. 'Yes! Ah, yes! Of course! You don't know, do you?'

'Know what?' said Dougal, icily.

'No, of course you wouldn't know!' said Brian. 'How could you?! Silly of me!'

Dougal waited.

'Ha! Ha!' laughed Brian. 'I am a potty old thing!
What must you think of me?'

'Do you really want to know?' said Dougal.

'Ha! Ha!' laughed Brian again, just a little nervously.
'Ha! Ha! Ha!'

He took a sip of tea and a deep breath.

'You're taking us all on holiday this winter,' he said,
very quickly.

Dougal dropped his cup on the floor.

'You've dropped your cup, old mate,' said Brian.

'*What* did you say?' said Dougal.

'I said you've dropped your cup,' said Brian.

'Before that,' said Dougal.

'Before that? said Brian. 'Ah! Now you're asking me
to remember. Before that . . . hmm . . . what did I say?'

'Yes, what?' said Dougal.

'Ooh, difficult to remember,' said Brian. 'Difficult to
make the old brain tick over.'

'Force yourself,' said Dougal.

'Er . . . was it about winter?' said Brian.

'Yes,' said Dougal.

'And a holiday?' said Brian.

'Yes,' said Dougal.

'About winter and a holiday?' said Brian.

'Yes,' said Dougal.

'Could it have been about you taking us all on holiday this winter?' said Brian.

Dougal dropped his saucer.

'You've dropped your saucer, old thing,' said Brian.

'I KNOW!!' screeched Dougal. 'I KNOW!! I
KNOW!! *I KNOW*!!' And he picked up the cup and
saucer, dropped them again, kicked them across the

room and jumped on to a chair.

'I KNOW!!'

'Well, that's all right then if you know,' said Brian. 'Can I have another cup of tea?'

Dougal sat down heavily.

'Pour me one,' he said, 'and tell me the worst.'

'Well,' said Brian, 'we thought it would be lovely to have a winter holiday this year and as you're so good at organising things we thought you would make all the arrangements and take us.'

'Who's we?' said Dougal.

'Florence and me,' said Brian, '. . . and Mr Rusty and Mr MacHenry.'

'Anyone else?' said Dougal.

'Dylan,' said Brian.

'And?' said Dougal.

'Ermintrude,' said Brian.

Dougal groaned.

'What have I done to deserve it?' he said.

Brian finished his tea.

'Well, that's all settled then,' he said. 'I can leave the arrangements to you . . . all right?'

'No, it's not all right!' said Dougal.

'Where are you taking us?' said Brian, brightly.

'Give me time to *think*,' said Dougal, '. . . per-lease!!'

'Of course,' said Brian. 'I'll get the others and we'll come back in . . . what? Ten minutes?'

'Make it three days,' said Dougal, 'and not a minute sooner.'

'They're very impatient to start,' said Brian.

'Then tell them to start,' said Dougal. '*I* shan't mind.'

'Without you?' said Brian. 'Our leader, our friend and

holiday arranger . . .'

'Get out!' said Dougal.

'Any tea left?' said Brian.

'GET OUT!!' said Dougal, and Brian got out.

Dougal sat down and thought. He thought it was rotten of everyone to expect him to arrange their holidays. He thought that a holiday, however, might be rather nice, especially in the winter. So he thought about what sort of holiday it should be.

'Winter,' he mused. 'Where can you go in the winter? It's so *cold* . . .'

He stopped.

'Snow?' he thought. 'That's it! A holiday with snow.' He rushed about.

'What a great notion! And the very place? *Scotland*! Plenty of snow! I'll take them to my Uncle Hamish in Glen Dougal and introduce them to the clan! With any luck I may lose the lot of them in a drift.'

He chortled and ran round in a circle nine times.

'*Scotland the Brave*,' he sang. 'Now where are my skis . . . and my haggis bag, and my skates and the woolly cap my Auntie Megsie knitted?'

He threw things out of drawers and hunted in cupboards.

'*Scotland the Brave*,' he sang . . .

The winter holiday was decided.

# It is arranged

Dougal's room was crowded. Everyone was there, sitting wherever there was room. Florence, Brian, Mr MacHenry, Mr Rusty, Dylan and, half in and half out because of space problems, Ermintrude.

'Now are we all here?' said Dougal. He was wearing a tartan tammy and looked quite imposing. 'Is everyone *assembled*?'

'More or less, dear thing,' said Ermintrude. 'And we're all *agog*, aren't we?'

Everyone agreed that they were about as agog as they could get.

'I'm so agog I'm *hot*,' said Brian.

'Try getting off the stove,' said Dougal.

'Eek!' said Brian, getting off.

'Try not to interrupt too much, Brian,' murmured Florence.

Dougal took up an important position, adjusted his tammy and told them his plan.

They were to go to Scotland. Everyone would be accommodated with Dougal's Uncle Hamish, who had a large house. Dougal had sent a telegram to tell him they were coming, and everyone would assemble to leave, ready packed, in an hour's time.

Everyone started to talk at once. How could they go to Scotland? How would they know what to wear? How could they be ready in an hour's time?

'Silence!' shouted Dougal.

There was silence.

'I don't know what all the fuss is about,' he said. '*I'm* ready to leave.'

'But you *knew*!' they shrieked.

'All right! All right!' said Dougal. 'Just get ready as quickly as you can and we'll start.'

'Right!' said Florence. 'Everyone get ready.'

'EVERYONE GET READY!' shouted Brian. 'AND WE'LL START!'

They all went to get ready.

'Don't be long!' shouted Dougal.

'We won't,' they shouted back.

And they weren't. Much sooner than Dougal had expected they were all back, loaded with luggage and expectation.

Mr MacHenry was wearing an overcoat and a muffler, and carrying a canvas bag marked 'Epton MacHenry – Botanist'.

Mr Rusty also had an overcoat and a muffler and was dragging a large trunk labelled 'S.S. Titanic – THIS SIDE UP'.

Ermintrude had on a new hat covered in plastic daisies and was carrying a net full of hay with a large label on it saying 'HAY'.

Dylan was carrying a guitar, a rucksack and a large bunch of carrots.

Florence had a brand new ribbon in her hair and was carrying a school satchel marked 'FLORENCE –

TOP IN GEOG' in red ink. She also had a very large basket labelled 'LUNCHEON'.

Brian had a blue case marked 'SAVOY HOTEL – LAUNDRY' and a large bag of lettuces.

He dumped these on Dougal's doorstep.

'How do we get there then?' he said.

Dougal paled.

'What?' he said, faintly.

'Oh, sorry,' said Brian, brightly, 'have I asked an awkward question?'

'Of course you haven't, Brian,' said Florence.

She turned to Dougal. His tammy had slipped right over his eyes and he seemed to be having difficulty breathing.

'Well?' she said.

Dougal opened his mouth to speak, but no sound came out except a high-pitched squeak.

'Are you all right, Dougal?' asked Florence, but before he could reply there was a loud whistle and a train arrived outside with a clank and a whoosh.

'You weren't thinking of leaving without me, were you?' she hissed.

'NO!!' said Dougal, so loudly they all jumped. 'No!! No!! Of course not! You're taking us all to Scotland on holiday, remember?'

'Scotland? Holiday?' said the train. 'I never . . . '

But before she could say another word, Dougal started to bundle everyone in.

'Come along! Come along! Don't dawdle! We'll never get there!' he shouted.

The train gave a very loud whistle. Everyone stopped.

'Now just a little moment,' said the train. 'If I'm taking you all to Scotland, one or two requirements have to be met. There are certain *rules* for journeys and I don't move a single puff without them. First I shall need a guard . . .'

'Me!' said Mr Rusty. 'I've always wanted to be a guard – man and boy.'

'Good! OFF WE GO!' shouted Dougal.

The train whistled again.

'Not so fast,' she said. 'I need a ticket collector and a buffet attendant and a stoker and a chum to talk to during the dreary bits.'

Dougal groaned quietly.

'Be quicker by bicycle at this rate,' he muttered.

Dylan was chosen ticket collector.

Brian was elected stoker.

Mr MacHenry volunteered to ride up front and talk to the train when necessary.

All that was needed then was a cook and buffet attendant.

Everyone looked at Florence.

'Why are you all looking at me? she said.

'You're a lady,' they said, 'and so a born provider.'

Florence sighed.

'Oh, all right,' she said. 'But don't expect too much.'

They all prepared to get on board, but Dougal made them wait while he went along the train painting big numbers on each carriage.

1        2        3        4

'What *are* you doing, Dougal!' they asked.

Dougal got in the carriage marked 1.

'You don't expect me to travel Second Class, do you?' he said.

'What about us?' they said.

'It's very simple,' said Dougal. 'As leader and thinker I travel First Class. Miss Florence as cook and lady travels Second. Rabbits traditionally go Third, Mr MacHenry travels in the front and Mr Rusty in the guard's van.'

'What about pretty brown-eyed me?' said Brian.

'For you,' said Dougal, 'a special class has been created. It has never been used before – not even on the mail train to Siberia – FOURTH!'

'You're too good to me,' said Brian.

'Oh, get in,' said Dougal, 'and don't put your feet on the seat.'

'I haven't got any feet,' said Brian.

'Stop arguing!' shouted Dougal. 'All aboard! Here we go! Scots wha' hae!'

'Er . . . Excuse me,' said Ermintrude, 'but I appear to have been overlooked.'

The train gave a toot and started to move.

'You're going without me!' wailed Ermintrude.

Everyone except Dougal leaned out of the windows and urged Ermintrude to get in before it was too late.

'But *where* shall I get in?' she puffed, running alongside.

'Anywhere!' they said.

So Ermintrude opened a door and got in.

'WHAT!! WHAT!! WHAT!!' screeched Dougal. 'COWS DO NOT TRAVEL FIRST!!'

'Too late!' they cried. 'We're moving.'

Dougal put his head out of the window.

'STOP!' he cried.

'TOO LATE!' they shouted.

'TOOT! TOOT!' went the train.

Dougal sighed, and sat down.

'How long is the journey, dear thing?' said Ermintrude.

'I don't know,' sighed Dougal, 'but it's going to seem long.'

'St George for England; St Pancras for Scotland!' sang the train.

# *The Journey*

They left the garden and started the journey to Scotland. It was a good moment, like so many starts. Brian, stoking like anything, sang a song which sounded like: *Good thing Wendy's mouse looks stout*, but probably wasn't.

Florence was preparing lunch. She was a bit worried because she didn't have enough fish fingers for seven, but, as she said to herself, they could make up with a lot of mashed potato.

Mr MacHenry was listening to Brian singing and asking the train every now and again if she was all right.

The train *was* all right and enjoying the scenery around Watford.

Mr Rusty was busy guarding, looking out at every station and hoping they might stop so that he could do a bit of flag-waving.

Dylan had decided that as no one was paying there was no need to collect tickets, so he was sleeping instead.

Ermintrude was singing selections from *Carmen*.

Dougal was looking out of the window.

'What have I done to deserve it?' he thought.

But by and large it was a happy trainful and it seemed

as though the journey to Scotland would be completed in record time.

At Crewe, while the train filled herself with what she assured everyone was water, Florence served a light luncheon. Afterwards, she made tea and lemonade and they all sat in the buffet car talking about the journey.

'I should like to make absolutely certain of the route,' said Mr Rusty, 'so that I know if we go wrong or not.'

'How can we go wrong?' said Florence.

'We just keep going on up, don't we?'

'Can't be too careful,' said Mr Rusty. 'Now, what are the main stops?'

Dougal consulted a little map on the wall.

'It's quite simple,' he said. 'It's CREWE (we've been there), CARLISLE, GLASGOW, AUCHEN-SHUGGLE, TILLIETUDLEM, GLENGOE and

GLEN DOUGAL.'
 'BRISTOL! BRISTOL!' shouted a voice outside.
'BRISTOL!'

'Bristol?!' said Dougal, faintly.
'Bristol?' said Mr MacHenry.
'I warned you,' said Mr Rusty.
Dougal rushed to the window and looked out. A

porter was walking along the platform.

'Er . . . excuse me,' said Dougal. 'Is this Bristol?'

'Oh, no, me dear,' said the porter. 'It's Bognor Regis. I'm just shoutin' Bristol 'cos I likes the name.'

'Well, there's no need for sarcasm,' said Dougal, tartly.

'An' there's no need for soppy questions either,' said the porter, going away.

Dougal pulled his head back in.

'Now there's no need to panic,' he said. 'We musn't panic.'

'We have no intention of panicking, dear thing,' said Ermintrude. 'Why should we?'

'Er . . . I'll go and see what's happening,' said Mr Rusty. 'It's my duty.' And he went.

'I expect there's a perfectly simple explanation,' said Florence.

There was. Mr Rusty came back and explained that the train had taken a little detour to see a friend of hers who was about to retire from the railway service.

'We'll be going again soon,' he said.

'I don't know,' said Dougal, irritably. 'What a way to run a railway!'

'Don't worry,' said Florence.

'Don't worry?! Don't worry?!' said Dougal. 'Someone's got to worry. It would be a fine thing if nobody worried, wouldn't it?'

'Well, worrying won't start the train,' said Florence.

There was a jerk and the train started. Dougal looked at Florence.

'When's tea?' he said.

'I'll make it now,' sighed Florence.

The train went on while they all had tea. They

discussed how long it might take to get to Scotland now
that they'd detoured to Bristol. Dougal and Mr Rusty
were a bit pessimistic but, as Florence said, the train was
going very fast and they weren't likely to go out of their
way again.

'I wish I could believe that,' said Dougal, gloomily.
'She's probably got a friend with 'flu at Aberystwyth.'

There was a jerk and a crash. The teacups scattered in
all directions. Dougal fell on top of Brian. Dylan woke
up and everyone else rolled about in all directions.

'What on earth's happening?' said Florence.

The train jerked and rolled and bumped.

'What's happening!?' shrieked Dougal.

They bumped and bumped and finally stopped.

'Listen!' said Mr MacHenry.

There was a noise, muffled and distant, but loud
enough for everyone to hear.

Herroooff! it sounded like.

'We must have hit something,' said Florence.

Herroooff!! went the noise again.

'I shall go and investigate again,' said Mr Rusty. 'It's
my duty.'

'I think we should all go,' said Florence, firmly. She
didn't like the sound of that 'Herroooff!'

Herroooff!

The noise happened again, and this time it seemed a
bit nearer.

'Listen,' whispered Dougal.

They all listened.

Herroooff!

'I think it's in here,' said Florence, faintly.

Herroooff!!

'It's near you, Dougal,' said Florence.

'What!' screeched Dougal, leaping up.

There was Brian, looking a bit squashed and a lot annoyed.

'Thank you,' he said. 'Too kind. Didn't you hear me shouting, you great woolly thing?'

'Steady, Brian,' said Florence.

'I'll never be steady again,' said Brian. 'I'm a squashed snail.'

'Do you good,' said Dougal, heartlessly.

'Oh, get off!' said Brian, and he went and sat down in a corner, looking like a snail who had been sat on by a dog.

The others, led by Dougal, went to see the train. They were in the middle of a field, and the train looked very disconsolate.

'I went off the rails,' she said, faintly. 'Is everyone all right?'

They assured her they were and helped her back on, Dougal leading the way and the others pushing and grunting. When she was back, Florence went to see her.

'All right now?' she asked. 'Pointing the right way?'

'Quite the right way, I think,' said the train, and she gave a little toot.

'All aboard,' said Mr Rusty, waving his flag. Everyone got aboard and they started again.

'We'll take days at this rate,' said Dougal.

'I'm squashed,' moaned Brian.

'Then you won't want any cake, will you?' said Florence, briskly.

'I might force down a small piece,' said Brian.

So they all had some more tea and cake while the train went on.

They passed Carlisle safely. Then Glasgow.

'The Eternal City,' breathed Dougal, looking out.

Then Auchenshuggle.

Then Tillietudlum . . .

Dougal began to get excited.

'Glencoe!' he said. 'Oh, the beauty of it.'

He opened the window.

'Curse ye, Black Campbells!' he shrieked.

'Dougal, please!' said Florence.

'Sorry,' said Dougal. 'I was overcome.'

The train slowed. She gave a little toot. Dougal rushed to the window again.

'We've arrived!' he shouted. 'We've arrived! Oh, I'm so happy!'

'I'm squashed,' said Brian.

'Oh, be quiet!' they all shouted, rushing to the windows and looking out.

The train was pulling into a small station. All around was snow and the big hills were covered in pine trees all with snow on them like thousands of Christmas trees.

'It's beautiful,' breathed Florence.

'Home!' said Dougal.

'Squashed,' said Brian.

The train stopped with a hiss. Everything was quiet. Then from the far end of the platform came a sound . . . a musical sound.

'The pipes!' whispered Dougal. 'Oh, the pipes! I may cry!'

They all got out and stood on the platform. Coming towards them, wearing a kilt and a large plaid bonnet and playing a set of bagpipes, was a small, black figure.

'Uncle Hamish,' breathed Dougal.

# Scotland

Uncle Hamish advanced on them playing the pipes louder and louder until finally, just as he arrived, he stopped playing and there was silence.

He fixed them all with glittering eyes.

'Where's wee Dougie?' he said, very loudly.

Everyone jumped and Mr Rusty laughed nervously.

'Wee Dougie's here,' said Brian, pushing Dougal forward with his nose.

Uncle Hamish looked at Dougal.

'Ye're late!' he said. 'Ye'll get no tea. And put your tammy straight – ye look like Harry Lauder's mother. Come!'

And he put the bag of his bagpipes under his arm, blew powerfully, went quite red in the face and stumped away down the platform, the pipes wailing.

Dougal looked at the others.

'He's all right really,' he said, laughing nervously. 'It's just his way.'

'Lead on, wee Dougie,' said Brian.

'Any trouble out of you and I'll feed you to a Highland cow,' said Dougal.

'Oh, any about? mooed Ermintrude.

'I think we'd better go before Uncle Hamish gets

cross,' said Florence, and they all followed Dougal down the platform.

Uncle Hamish was waiting beside a huge, black open car covered with stickers saying 'Prevent Forest Fires'.

'Get in, get in,' he said, and they all got in.

'Ye'd better sit beside me, lassie,' he said to Florence.

Florence sat in the front seat while Uncle Hamish covered her right up to the chin with a tartan rug.

'Everyone ready?' he asked.

They were.

Uncle Hamish started the engine, put the car into gear, looked round at Florence, gave a huge wink and they were off.

Florence sat back.

'It's going to be all right,' she thought.

They drove away from the station and down a little lane on to the main road. It was getting dark and a light snow began to fall.

'Is it far?' asked Florence.

'Just a step,' said Uncle Hamish. 'Sixty miles.' And he gave Florence another huge wink.

'Sixty miles!' said Mr Rusty.

'Just a step?' said Mr MacHenry.

'We'll be frozen solid!' said Dougal.

'If ye'd rather walk, ye can!' said Uncle Hamish, turning round and glittering at Dougal.

'Uncle . . . please, *please* look where you're going,' said Dougal, nervously.

Uncle Hamish turned back and stared down the road.

'No, one would be foolish enough to get in *my* way,' he said.

'Not even trees?' said Brian, brightly, but Uncle

Hamish was turning left through some huge iron gates.

'We're there,' he said.

'Sixty miles already?' said Ermintrude.

'My little joke,' boomed Uncle Hamish. 'Ha! Ha!'

He turned and looked at them.

'Ha! Ha!' they said, nervously.

The car pulled up in front of a huge, grey turreted house and they all got out clutching their luggage.

'Angus!' shouted Uncle Hamish, in a voice that would have penetrated lead. 'Where are ye, ye lop-sided lump of rubbish?!'

The great front door creaked open and out of it came a hugh Highland bull. His horns measured a good six feet across and his eyes were completely covered in a mat of light brown hair.

'Ah, hush yer whisht!' he said.

'Dinna hush yer whisht to me!' shouted Uncle Hamish.

'And dinna shout at me, ye wee black bannock!' bellowed Angus.

'Get my friends inside!' screeched Uncle Hamish.

'Why, are they all helpless?' boomed Angus.

'I think we'd better go in,' whispered Florence, and she went up the front steps followed by the others.

Ermintrude was last. She passed Angus.

'Halloo,' she said.

Angus stopped glowering at Uncle Hamish and looked at Ermintrude.

'Eh . . . let me carry you hay for ye, m'dear,' he said.

'Too kind,' murmured Ermintrude.

They all stood in the great hall. A huge fire was burning huge logs in the huge fireplace.

'Ye'll find your rooms marked clearly,' said Uncle Hamish.

'But first I expect ye'd like a little something?'

'Well, it has been a long day,' said Florence.

'Ye poor wee creatures,' said Uncle Hamish. 'ANGUS!! OPEN THE DOOR!!'

Angus walked slowly down the hall and pushed open a door. There, in a huge dining room with another huge fire burning more huge logs was a huge table laid with a huge meal. There was scones and potatoes and pies and cakes and carrots and lettuce and ice-cream and big pots of tea.

'Better get to it,' said Uncle Hamish, 'before it gets spoiled.'

So they all sat down to one of the best meals they'd ever had in their lives and afterwards they were very ready for bed.

Next morning Florence woke up very early. The frost had made patterns on her window and from outside came the sound of bagpipes. She went across to the window, rubbed a little hole to see through, and looked out. There was Uncle Hamish walking up and down in the snow playing his pipes.

'Goodness, he must be cold,' thought Florence.

There was a great booming clanging noise outside the door. She peeped out. Angus was walking slowly along the corridor banging a gong strung between his horns. All down the corridor doors opened and heads peered out.

'Breakfast!' bellowed Angus, banging his way down the stairs.

And they all went down to breakfast.

Uncle Hamish came in and sat down at the head of the table.

'After ye've eaten,' he said, 'I want ye all changed into civilised apparal. And that means the kilt. Which tartan d'ye wear?'

He looked at them fiercely.

'Er . . . is there a MacCow?' said Ermintrude, nervously.

Uncle Hamish took a deep breath.

'Nay, there is not,' he said. 'Ye'll wear the Angus. What about you?' he said to Brian.

Brian choked on a cornflake.

'MacDougal,' he squeaked. 'What else?'

'Ye'll go far,' said Uncle Hamish.

He looked around.

'MacHenry,' said Mr MacHenry.

'There's no such clan,' said Uncle Hamish. He thought. 'Ye're never Irish, are ye?'

'It is possible,' said Mr MacHenry.

Uncle Hamish sighed.

'I can see it's little use,' he said. 'Ye'll all have to wear the true tartan. I've got a few in the great cupboard. Put them on.'

He drank a cup of tea, ate seven kippers in quick succession and stumped out.

'He's a character,' said Mr Rusty.

'He is that,' said Mr MacHenry, and after breakfast they all dressed themselves in the true tartan. Brian had a little difficulty because of his lack of waist and legs, but they finally all assembled in the great hall and waited for anything that might happen.

Uncle Hamish came in. Behind him was Angus with a bag and a hamper.

'All set then?' said Uncle Hamish.

'Er . . . for what, Uncle Hamish?' said Dougal.

'Well, 'tis Tuesday,' said Uncle Hamish. 'And on Tuesdays, rain or shine, snow or sleet, sun or typhoon, we hunt the haggis.'

'Er . . . will we be back for lunch?' said Dougal.

Uncle Hamish glittered.

'Can ye think of nothing but your tum, laddie?' he roared. 'Come, we're away.'

'How exciting,' breathed Florence.

Mr MacHenry asked if it would be all right for him to be excused the haggis hunt; he would prefer to look around the gardens. Mr Rusty said that would suit him better too.

'Please yourselves,' said Uncle Hamish. 'Come, we're away.'

'Follow me, me dear,' whispered Angus to Ermintrude. 'I've got a picnic basket.'

'What are ye whispering about, ye great lummock?' roared Uncle Hamish.

'Ah, hist!' said Angus. 'Can I not whisper now?'

Uncle Hamish glowered.

'Come, we're away,' he said.

'How exciting,' breathed Florence.

And they set off on the haggis hunt.

# Haggis hunt

Outside, Uncle Hamish stood by a large open cart. Harnessed to the cart was a horse smoking a long cigar. He had one front leg crossed over the other and looked a bit bored.

'Come away, all,' shouted Uncle Hamish, and they all got into the cart.

'Up! Up! Big John,' said Uncle Hamish. The horse uncrossed his legs and began to pull the cart very slowly down the drive towards the big iron gates.

'Big John!' shouted Uncle Hamish, 'I'll trouble ye to break into a trot.'

The horse looked over his shoulder.

'That'll be the day,' he drawled, going slowly on. Uncle Hamish glowered but said nothing.

'Why's he called Big John?' whispered Florence.

'Ah, now,' said Uncle Hamish, loudly. 'He was once in a Cowboy and Indian film and he's never been the same since.'

'Get away,' said Big John.

The cart moved slowly along the road through the snow; Florence in the front with Uncle Hamish; Brian, Dougal and Dylan in the middle; and Angus and Ermintrude sitting on the picnic basket at the back, giggling a lot.

They turned off the road through a gate marked 'No Trespassers – No Campbells'.

'Why does it say "No Campbells", Uncle Hamish?' asked Florence.

'I'll not have a Campbell on my land,' said Uncle Hamish, sternly.

'Why?' said Florence.

'Because they're black-hearted, fierce and untrustworthy,' said Uncle Hamish.

'Oh,' said Florence.

They went along a lane through dark pine woods. The lane went up and up, twisting and turning until it reached the end of the trees and there, by a big dead pine, they stopped.

'We start here,' said Uncle Hamish, unhitching Big John and giving him a nosebag. 'Out, everybody.'

Dylan had fallen asleep in the bottom of the cart, but everyone else got out.

'We'll go in two's,' said Uncle Hamish. 'Ye'll come with me, lassie,' he said to Florence.

'And ye'll come with me, lassie,' said Angus to Ermintrude.

Brian turned to Dougal.

'Don't say it!' said Dougal. 'My first haggis hunt,' he groaned, 'and I'm saddled with a snail.'

'What about Dylan?' said Florence.

'Yon rabbit can do as he pleases,' said Uncle Hamish, and as Dylan seemed pleased to sleep, they left him.

'We'll go three ways and meet back here for lunch,' said Uncle Hamish. 'Take care the wee beasties don't outfox ye.' And he set off with Florence at a brisk trot.

Angus and Ermintrude went another way, not quite so briskly, and Brian looked at Dougal again.

'Have you even the remotest idea what to do?' he asked, brightly.

'No, I haven't,' said Dougal, crossly.

Big John looked over his nosebag.

'You need to creep up and surround them,' he drawled.

'How can I creep up and surround them?' said Dougal. 'I don't even know what they look like.'

'Oh,' said Big John, 'you can't miss them. They're round and fat and they go "whee!" a lot.'

'They sound lovely,' said Brian. 'Are there many about?'

'Something like two million at the last count,' said Big John.

'Not dangerous, I take it,' said Dougal, casually.

'Depends,' said Big John, laconically.

'On what?' said Dougal, nervously.

'On whether they're crept up on and surrounded,' said Big John, and he closed both eyes and sat down.

'Oh, well, better show willing, I suppose,' said Brian. 'Come on.'

'I've gone off the whole idea, but Uncle Hamish will expect me to catch one, I suppose,' said Dougal, and he followed Brian through the snow and up the hill.

Brian was enjoying himself. He slid uphill and he slid downhill. Dougal plodded along behind, his sporran full of snow and the fringes of his kilt covered with icicles. His head was low and his eyes on the ground.

'Whee!' said Brian, going down a little hill.

'Take cover!' screeched Dougal, going head first into a drift.

Brian came back.

'What are you doing in there?' he asked.

'I heard one,' said Dougal. 'It went "whee!"'

'Oh, sorry, that was me,' said Brian.

Dougal pulled himself out of the snow and shook.

'And why, pray, were you going "whee!"?' he asked.

'I just felt like it,' said Brian.

'Well, the next time you feel like it, let me know,' said Dougal.

'Carry me then,' said Brian.

'Certainly not,' said Dougal.

They went on. The snow got deeper and the hill got steeper.

Suddenly, 'whee! whee!' they heard.

'Was that you?' whispered Dougal.

'No,' whispered Brian.

'Whee! whee!' they heard again.

Dougal went whiter than the snow.

'It's a haggis,' he said, faintly.

'Whee! whee!'

'And it's coming this way,' said Brian.

'Whee! whee! WHEEEE!!!'

A small, round tartan object hurtled over their heads and landed in a flurry of snow a few feet away.

It moved a little, and then was still.

Dougal and Brian moved towards it.

'Not very big,' whispered Brian.

'Whee!' it said suddenly, and Dougal and Brian somersaulted backwards into the soft snow.

The haggis looked at them with two piercing black eyes.

'Ye're not much good at it, are ye?' it said. 'Ye're supposed to creep up and surround me. I heard ye coming two miles awa'.'

'We've never done it before,' said Brian. 'Sir.'

'I can well tell you,' said the haggis. 'Are ye with Hamish's lot?'

Dougal and Brian confessed that they were.

'Aye, yon Hamish,' said the haggis, wheezing with laughter. 'Fifty years after the haggis and he's never caught one yet.'

'Have we caught you?' said Brian.

'Ye have *not*,' said the haggis, 'but you're welcome to try. You know to creep up and surround me.'

'So we understand,' said Dougal.

'What happens if we do?' said Brian.

'Then I'm captured,' said the haggis.

'And if we don't?' said Dougal, nervously.

'Then ye have to go to Oban for a new haggis-hunting licence,' said the haggis. 'And Oban's a long way,' it wheezed. 'Are ye ready?'

They said they were.

'Away we go then,' said the haggis, and it shot straight up in the air with a 'whee' and disappeared like a bullet in the direction of Norway.

Dougal sat down.

'This is hopeless,' he said. 'It's about a hundred miles away by now and I'm *cold*.'

'We don't want to be thought failures though, do we?' said Brian.

'Why not?' said Dougal.

'That's not the attitude,' said Brian, sternly. 'Come on, old chum. Up! Up! Deep breaths!'

'Oh, stop being so outdoor and hearty,' said Dougal.

Brian climbed up a little hill and slid down again.

'I've got a marvellous idea,' he said. 'We'll *make* one.'

'We'll *what*?' said Dougal.

'Make a haggis,' said Brian, 'and pretend we crept up on it and surrounded it and captured it. Get your kilt off.'

'I will not! said Dougal. 'The idea . . .'

'This is no time for arguing,' said Brian. 'Get it off!'

'Only under protest,' said Dougal with dignity, and he took his kilt off and gave it to Brian.

Brian spread it on the ground and pushed snow into it.

'Pat it so that it's round,' he said.

'You pat it,' said Dougal. 'I provided the kilt.'

'I can't pat without hands,' said Brian, with exasperation. 'I'm doing this for *you*, you know.'

'I'm truly grateful,' said Dougal, sarcastically. But he patted the snow into a round ball and fastened the kilt round it. It looked just like a haggis except for the eyes.

'What about the eyes?' he said.

'Paint!' said Brian.

'Brilliant!' said Dougal. 'It just so happens I have a gallon of paint in me sporran. Great clump!'

'Don't be like that,' said Brian, and he burrowed into the snow until he had cleared a little patch.

'We'll use mud,' he said. 'Sit down here.'

'Why?' said Dougal.

'The ground's frozen – we'll have to warm it,' said Brian.

Dougal sat down.

'The things I do,' he said, heavily.

Meanwhile, back at the cart, the others had returned from the haggis hunt empty-handed. They sat down while Angus spread the picnic and soon they were all eating huge sandwiches and drinking bottles of milk.

'Didn't catch many, did we?' said Florence, brightly.

'Nay,' said Uncle Hamish, gloomily.

'Do you usually catch a lot?' said Florence.

'Nay,' said Uncle Hamish.

'What's the most you've ever caught?' said Florence.

'He's never caught one,' bellowed Angus. 'Never a one!'

'Silence, ye crummock!' shouted Uncle Hamish.

'Ha!' scoffed Angus. 'Never a one!'

'I wonder where Dougal and Brian have got to?' said Florence, trying to change the subject.

'Up to their sporrans in a drift, I shouldn't wonder,' said Uncle Hamish. 'Pass the sandwiches, lassie.'

There was a shout. Dougal and Brian appeared on the brow of the hill holding something up.

'I think they've caught one,' breathed Florence. 'How exciting.'

'Aye,' said Uncle Hamish, not appearing to be too pleased.

Dougal and Brian arrived breathless.

'Where's your kilt, Dougal?' said Florence.

'I lost it in the battle with this haggis,' said Dougal, quickly.

'Ye got one then?' said Uncle Hamish, slowly.

'Yes,' said Dougal.

'Aye,' said Brian.

Uncle Hamish inspected the haggis Brian and Dougal had brought.

'Aye,' he said. 'A good specimen. We'll hang it in the hall over the great fire. Aye.'

Dougal went pale and choked on a sandwich.

'Over the great fire?' said Brian.

'Aye,' said Uncle Hamish. ''Tis the first and it shall have the place of honour next to the salmon caught on the Tay in '89 by Queen Victoria.'

'Er . . . Uncle Hamish,' said Dougal. 'Shouldn't we just let it go perhaps?'

'Let it go!' shouted Uncle Hamish. 'My first haggis?'

'We caught it,' squeaked Brian.

'On *my* land,' said Uncle Hamish, sternly, 'and on the wall over the fire it shall go. Come, we'll be away back.'

They packed up the picnic and all got into the cart, Uncle Hamish putting the haggis under his seat.

'Now, Big John,' he said. 'Home – at a gallop.'

'That'll be the day,' said Big John, pulling the cart slowly away down the lane.

Dougal and Brian sat together nervously while the cart jolted along.

'Fine mess you've got me into,' muttered Dougal.

'I did my best,' murmured Brian.

'What's that . . . like . . . muttering?' said Dylan, waking up. 'Have I missed anything?'

'Oh, go back to sleep,' said Dougal.

'I will, man,' said Dylan, and he pulled the haggis out from under the seat, put his head on it and went to sleep again.

They jogged on.

Suddenly Brian nudged Dougal.

'Look!' he whispered.

'Oh, my,' said Dougal, looking.

A trickle of water was running along the bottom of the cart. It was the haggis, melting rapidly.

'He's melting it,' said Brian. 'Quick, get it out.'

Dougal pulled the haggis out from under Dylan's head. It unrolled completely, and a ball of squashy snow tumbled slowly off the back of the cart.

'What shall we do?' moaned Dougal.

'Put the kilt on,' whispered Brian, urgently.

'It's all soggy,' hissed Dougal.

'Never mind that,' said Brian.

Dougal put his wet kilt back on and waited apprehensively as they jogged along.

When they got back it was getting dark. Uncle Hamish got down and reached under the seat. He fumbled and felt.

'It's gone!' he thundered.

'Gone?' said Florence.

'Gone?' said Dougal, in a high-pitched voice.

'I *thought* I heard a "whee!"' said Brian.

Uncle Hamish was silent for a moment and then he said in a voice which seemed quite pleased, 'Ah, well! They're cunning wee beasties. Come, we'll have some tea.'

'I see you got your kilt back, Dougal,' whispered Florence, significantly.

'Don't be rotten,' said Dougal, and they all went in to tea.

# Tobogganing

At breakfast next morning no mention was made of the haggis hunt. Instead, after his usual batch of kippers, Uncle Hamish suggested they might like to amuse themselves as he was going to be busy.

'I've work to do,' he said, 'but ye'll find plenty of diversion, I've no doubt.'

Florence assured him that they would and he wasn't to worry about them.

'Och, I'll not worry about ye,' said Uncle Hamish, stumping off. 'Enjoy yourselves.'

They sat round the table wondering what to do.

'If we had some skis, we could ski,' said Florence.

'If we had a toboggan, we could toboggan,' said Ermintrude.

'If we had some ice-skates, we could ice-skate,' said Mr MacHenry.

'And if we had any sense we could think of something,' said Brian.

'All right, clever breeks,' said Dougal, '*you* think of something.'

'I have,' said Brian.

They waited. Brian buttered a piece of toast.

'Well, tell us then!' said Dougal, furiously.

'Plead with me,' said Brian.

'Really, you are *impossible*,' said Dougal. 'And you've got butter all over your nose.'

'Perhaps if you *could* tell us Brian . . . ?' said Florence.

Brian rubbed his nose on the tablecloth to wipe the butter off.

'Has it gone?' he asked.

They assured him it had and waited, expectantly.

'Tin trays,' said Brian.

'Tin trays,' said Dougal.

'Tin trays,' said Brian. 'They make good toboggans . . . I remember.'

'Brian, you are clever,' said Florence.

'Huh! *Anyone* could have thought of *that*,' said Dougal.

'Then why didn't you?' said Florence.

'My mind was on higher things,' said Dougal, loftily, 'but I would have got round to it.'

'There's only one little problem as I see it, dear things,' said Ermintrude, 'and that is where to acquire these tin trays.'

'A house like this is sure to have tin trays,' said Mr Rusty. 'Houses like this always do.'

'Then we'll go on a search,' said Florence, 'and meet in the hall in ten minutes.'

'You're a born organiser, dear heart,' said Ermintrude. And they all left to look for tin trays.

Ten minutes later, in the hall, they were all assembled again.

Brian had a tin tray. It was marked 'Primrose Tea Rooms. Scones Four a Penny'.

Dougal also had a tray. It was long and thin and

covered with a picture of Skelmorlie in the autumn.

Florence had found a large biscuit tin just big enough to sit in and Dylan had the lid, also just big enough to sit in.

Mr Rusty and Mr MacHenry were very pleased with themselves because they had found four flat pieces of wood and were busy working out ways of attaching them to their feet with string.

Ermintrude had failed. She came in with a tin lid about ten centimetres across.

'I don't think it will hold me,' she said, sadly.

'I don't think a barn door would hold *you*,' giggled Dougal.

'Cheeky thing,' said Ermintrude. 'Just for that I shall ride with you.'

Dougal paled.

'We'll take turns,' he said, quickly.

So they all wrapped up warm and went out.

Outside, Big John was leaning nonchalantly against the wall.

'Hello, Big John,' said Florence.

'Hi!' said Big John. 'Going some place?'

'Tobogganing,' said Florence.

'Waal, that's nice,' said Big John. 'I reckon Ben Bumpy would be the best place.'

'What's Ben Bumpy?' said Florence.

'A mountain,' said Big John.

'Is it far, dear horse?' said Ermintrude.

''Bout half a mile,' said Big John. '. . . as the crow flies.'

'And as the dog trudges?' said Dougal.

''Bout four miles,' said Big John. 'Straight up.'

'That's not so good,' said Mr Rusty, 'Especially at my age.'

''Course, if I'd a mind, I could take you,' said Big John.

'And have you a mind?' said Brian, brightly.

'Might,' said Big John.

'I wonder how long this fascinating conversation will go on?' whispered Dougal.

'Hush, Dougal,' said Florence. 'We'd be grateful for a lift, Big John.'

'Hitch up then,' said Big John, and as he moved away from the wall they saw he had attached to his harness a long rope.

'An animated ski-lift,' said Dougal. 'Now I've seen everything.'

They sat on their various trays, stood on their various skis, caught hold of the rope and Big John started off, pulling them along like a giant tail.

'I'm having to walk,' wailed Ermintrude.

'Get on somewhere,' they shouted.

'Where?' said Ermintrude.

'Anywhere!' they said.

So Ermintrude got on.

'Comfy, dear heart?' she said.

'The things I suffer,' said Dougal.

And Big John pulled them four miles straight up Ben Bumpy.

At the top it was beautiful. The sun was shining and glancing on the snow and they could see the sea glittering a long way off.

'Aren't we lucky?' said Florence.

'Lucky?' said Dougal. 'I've just travelled four miles

with my bottom
in the snow.'

They stood at the top and
looked down.

'Er . . . who's going to be first?' said Mr
Rusty.

It seemed a long way and no one was very keen
to be first down.

Brian sat on his tray.

'I provided the notion,' he said, 'and I think someone
else should provide the first run.'

'You're absolutely right, mollusc,' said Dougal, evilly,
siding up behind Brian. 'Oops! I've slipped! Oh, dear!'
And he gave Brian a little push.

'Help!' said Brian. 'Helllllp . . .'

'Quite a good turn of speed,' said Dougal, giggling,
'for a snail.'

And he laughed so much he sat down heavily on his tray.

'Help!' he said. 'Helllllp . . .'

'I don't think he meant to do that,' said Ermintrude, watching Dougal disappear.

'Perhaps you'd all care for a snack while we wait for them?' said Mr MacHenry. 'I just happened to bring a little something with me.'

'How thoughtful,' murmured Florence.

Meanwhile, half-way down the slope, Dougal was catching up with Brian very rapidly. Brian was enjoying himself.

'Whee,' he shouted, 'Whee!!'

Dougal slid swiftly on.

'Get out of the way!' he screeched.

Brian looked round.

'Eek!' he squeaked. 'You're bearing down on me! I hate being beared down on!'

'I can't help it!' shouted Dougal. 'Get out of the way.'

'Steer round me!' shouted Brian.

'I can't!' screamed Dougal.

'But you're not trying!' shouted Brian.

Dougal got closer and closer. There was a sharp clang.

'Welcome aboard,' said Brian.

'Only half of me's aboard,' moaned Dougal.

'Well, you weren't fully invited,' said Brian.

Ahead of them a large mound of snow loomed up.

'We'll go over it!' shouted Brian, happily. They didn't go over it; they went into it.

The others, watching from the top of the hill, saw Dougal and Brian hit the bank of snow and disappear.

'They've disappeared,' said Mr MacHenry.

'Do you think they're all right?' said Florence, anxiously.

'Of course, dear heart,' said Ermintrude. 'It's very soft snow.'

'Well, I think I'm going to see,' said Florence bravely, and she got in her biscuit tin.

'Er . . . goodbye,' she said.

'Give them our love,' they said.

'Er . . . no one else coming?' said Florence.

'We don't think so,' they said.

'Er . . . I'll be going then,' said Florence.

'Goodbye,' they said, giving her a little push.

Meanwhile, back in the snow, Dougal and Brian looked around. They were in an icy cavern and there was a dark tunnel leading out of it.

'That's a very dark tunnel,' said Brian.

'Nervous, snail?' said Dougal.

'Yes,' said Brian, 'aren't you?'

'Certainly not,' said Dougal.

There was a snuffling, grunting noise from the tunnel.

'I am now,' said Dougal.

A long black and white nose appeared out of the tunnel, followed by a black and white head and a black and white body.

It was a badger.

'Can I help you?' he said, mildly.

'Well, not really,' said Brian, 'we . . . er . . . just dropped in.'

'I see you have a tray with you,' said the badger, 'and whilst this is not actually a cafeteria I could provide a cup of tea if you so wish.'

He disappeared down the tunnel.

'We've got a right one here,' whispered Dougal, and

he sat down very suddenly with a shriek as a biscuit tin hit him in the back.

'Hello,' said Florence. 'I was looking for you.'

'Just in time for tea,' said Brian.

Meanwhile, back on the hill, the others had watched Florence's progress with interest.

'The dear girl's disappeared too,' said Ermintrude. 'I think this now calls for a search party.'

'How many do you think constitutes a search party?' said Mr Rusty, nervously.

'Everyone,' said Ermintrude, firmly. 'Come along. Best feet forward.'

And she stepped on Mr Rusty's skis and slid rapidly down the hill.

'She's taken my skis, so I can't go,' said Mr Rusty.

'Borrow mine,' said Mr MacHenry.

'No, thank you,' said Mr Rusty.

But Dylan thought they should all go.

'Safety in numbers, men,' he said.

So on two skis and a biscuit tin lid they set out bravely.

Meanwhile, back in the badger's hallway, Florence and Brian and Dougal were drinking tea and the badger was apologising because he had no biscuits.

'I didn't expect anyone, you see,' he said.

'Please don't worry,' said Florence.

'Well, no, I won't worry,' said the badger. 'But I expect you were using the phrase politely because I imagine you wouldn't necessarily think that lack of biscuits would really tax my peace of mind . . .'

'He's off again,' whispered Dougal.

There was a flurry of snow and Ermintrude's head appeared.

'I'll just get another cup,' said the badger, and he went.

In quick succession Mr Rusty, Mr MacHenry and Dylan arrived in the icy hall.

'Bit crowded,' said Brian, taking the point of Mr Rusty's ski out of his ear.

The badger came back.

'Er . . . I hope we're not intruding?' said Mr Rusty.

'Intruding?' said the badger. 'Ah, now, well. Intrusion. To enter uninvited. To thrust oneself in forcibly and unwelcome. I suppose strictly speaking you have forced yourself in and you have entered uninvited, but as you are welcome I think we can safely say you are not intruding. I'll just get some more cups.'

'He must have a lot of cups,' said Brian.

They all had tea and the badger told them he lived alone and didn't see many strangers.

'I hope you will come again,' he said.

'Thank you,' said Florence. 'Er . . . I think we should go now.'

'Thank you for the tea,' they said.

'I'll just see you out,' said the badger.

Outside, Big John was waiting.

'Hello, Big John,' said the badger. 'Leg better?'

'Waal,' said Big John. 'It depends what you mean by better.'

'Let us say in the sense that it is not as bad as it was before,' said the badger.

'In that case, yes,' said Big John.

'Good,' said the badger.

'They do go on, don't they?' whispered Dougal.

'Just a tidge,' said Brian.

They all hitched up on Big John's rope and waved goodbye to the badger.

'Go safely,' he said.

'Goodbye, Mr Campbell,' said Big John.

And they all went home.

# *Golf*

One day, Brian and Dougal were having a look round in Uncle Hamish's loft. It was full of things and very dusty. There were dozens of old trunks and hatboxes, old broken chairs and cracked jugs, bundles of newspapers and boxes with string round them.

'What a great place,' said Brian, his head in a box.

Dougal sneezed.

'Oh, come out,' he said.

Brian came out and pounced on something lying in a corner.

'Hey, look!' he said. 'What's *this*?'

Dougal looked. It was a long bag and as Brian pulled it out, it rattled.

'That's a golf bag,' said Dougal, thoughtfully.

The bag had lots of little labels hanging from the handle. They read them.

'Hamish MacDougal. TROON 1923.'

'Hamish MacDougal. CARNOUSTIE 1931.'

'Hamish MacDougal. OPEN CHAMPION ST ANDREWS.'

'Open Champion!' breathed Dougal. 'Uncle Hamish! Well!'

'What's an Open Champion?' said Brian.

'It just means that Uncle Hamish was the best golfer in the world, that's all,' said Dougal. 'I wonder why he never told us?'

'Probably because we never asked him,' said Brian. 'Hey, why don't we have a game? Perhaps I could be Open Champion.'

'You couldn't be Open Champion if you were the only one playing,' said Dougal, scathingly.

'Let's play, anyway,' said Brian, 'it looks like a fun game.'

'It's not supposed to be *fun*,' said Dougal. 'It's *golf* and it's very *serious*.'

Uncle Hamish was in the hall when they went down with the golf clubs.

'Why didn't you tell us you were Open Champion?' said Dougal.

'I wasn't asked,' said Uncle Hamish.

'Will you have a game?' squeaked Brian.

Uncle Hamish looked the golf clubs over.

'Aye, it's been a long time,' he said, slowly. 'A long time since I played. ANGUS!!'

Angus appeared.

'Put out my plus-fours and my spikey shoes,' said Uncle Hamish, 'we're off to the links.'

Angus roared with laughter.

'At your age?' he bellowed. 'Ye'll not see the ball, let alone hit it!'

'Will ye do ye're told?' screamed Uncle Hamish. 'My plus-fours and my spikey shoes, if you please!!'

'I gave your plus-fours to the Women's Rural Jumble Sale twenty years ago,' said Angus, 'and your spikey shoes to Oxfam.'

'Ye'd no right!' screeched Uncle Hamish.

'Wear your brogues if ye're set on yon foolishness,' said Angus, picked up the clubs.

So Uncle Hamish put on his brogues and they set out for the golf course.

'I've never played golf,' said Brian, chattily.

'Then ye've never lived,' said Uncle Hamish.

They arrived at the course.

'Go into that shop,' said Uncle Hamish, 'say I sent you and ask Willie MacNuckle for some clubs to use.'

Dougal and Brian did so.

'This is a *shop*?' whispered Brian.

It was full of golf clubs and golf bags and golf balls and golf hats and golf woollies and golf umbellas.

'It's a *golf* shop,' whispered Dougal.

'I'd never have guessed,' giggled Brian.

'Nae giggling in my shop,' said a voice, sternly.

'Er . . . Mr MacNuckle?' said Dougal.

'Aye,' said Mr MacNuckle.

He was a little man with a huge red beard.

'Er . . . we want to borrow some clubs,' said Dougal.

'Uncle Hamish said you'd lend us some.'

'Do ye want a set each, or will one be enough?' he asked.

'Oh, I think one will be plenty,' said Brian. 'I'm not playing.'

'I'm relieved to hear that,' murmured Dougal.

Willie produced a set of clubs. Dougal picked them up and nearly fell over.

'They're a bit heavy,' he said.

Willie sighed.

'Would ye like a trolley?' he said.

'We'd love a trolley,' said Brian.

So Willie put the clubs on a little trolley and Dougal and Brian joined Uncle Hamish on the first tee, which was a little patch of grass.

Uncle Hamish walked on to it.

'Driver,' he said to Angus.

'Driver?' whispered Brian. 'Where's he going?'

'It's a golf club,' hissed Dougal.

Uncle Hamish put a ball on a little peg, gave a swish or two with his club and then hit the ball with a great crack. It shot away into the distance and Uncle Hamish strode away after it, followed by Angus who was muttering to himself.

'I think they've forgotten us,' said Brian, but they followed on with their bag and their trolley.

When they caught up, Uncle Hamish and Angus were looking at a little flag set on a stick about 175 yards away.

'Spoon,' said Uncle Hamish.

'Spoon?' said Angus. 'Are ye mad? Take the cleek.'

'Will ye give me the spoon and stop blethering!' screamed Uncle Hamish.

Angus silently gave Uncle Hamish a club and Uncle Hamish, after another swish or two, hit the ball another great crack. It soared up into the air and then came down, down, down and finally landed right beside the little flag.

Uncle Hamish gave the club back to Angus. Angus put the club in the bag.

'Ye'd have done better with the cleek,' he said, and they both strode away.

'Good game, isn't it?' said Brian, brightly.

'Oh, come on!' said Dougal.

They caught up again. Angus was holding the flag and Uncle Hamish was looking intently at his ball which was lying very close to a little hole.

'Er . . . Uncle Hamish . . .' said Dougal.

'Whisht!' said Uncle Hamish. 'I've a birdie here.'

'A birdie?' hissed Brian. 'Where?'

'How should I know?' said Dougal.

'Perhaps it's down the hole.'

Uncle Hamish walked round and looked at the ball from the other side.

'Och, get on with it,' murmured Angus, ''Tis dead.'

'A dead birdie?' whispered Brian. 'How sad.'

'I think it's golfing talk,' hissed Dougal.

Uncle Hamish finally made up his mind, took the club from the bag and, with a great indrawing of breath, tapped the ball into the hole.

'Lucky,' muttered Angus.

They walked off to another patch of grass.

'Er . . . Uncle Hamish,' said Dougal, but Uncle Hamish was busy studying another little flag – this time a much nearer one.

'Niblick?' said Angus. 'At your age? 'Tis a mashie-niblick at least.'

'Niblick!' roared Uncle Hamish.

'Ye're mad!' bellowed Angus.

'Will ye give me my niblick and stop chuntering?' said Uncle Hamish.

Angus silently gave Uncle Hamish a club.

'I find this quite fascinating,' whispered Brian.

Uncle Hamish swished the club again, gave a look towards the flag and hit the ball another great click. It sped up very high and came down again, bouncing on the green, this time hitting the flag-stick and stopping dead a short distance from the little hole.

Uncle Hamish handed the club back to Angus.

'Ye'd have done better wi' yer mashie-niblick,' said Angus.

'Ah, away with ye,' said Uncle Hamish, striding off.

'Do you think we should go home?' said Brian.

But Dougal was determined.

'Give me a club,' he said.

'You're never going to hit a ball,' said Brian, aghast.

'Yes, I am,' said Dougal. 'Give me a club.'

'Do you want a spoon, a cleek, a mashie or a baffy?' said Brian.

'Do you know which is which?' said Dougal, coldly.

'I could have a guess,' said Brian, happily.

'Oh, just give me one,' said Dougal.

Brian rummaged.

'There's a nice wooden one here,' he said.

'That'll do,' said Dougal, taking the club and walking on to the tee.

'I hope you know what you're doing,' said Brian, anxiously.

'Oh, be quiet,' said Dougal.

He set his ball on a little peg just as Uncle Hamish had done and took a swish or two.

'Watch where it goes!' he screamed, and aimed a great blow at the ball.

There was silence.

'Did you watch it?' asked Dougal.

'Yes,' said Brian.

'Then where did it go?' demanded Dougal.

'It's still there,' said Brian.

Dougal looked down.

'Well, watch it this time,' he muttered, 'and stop messing about.'

'Sorry,' said Brian.

Dougal took another swish or two, looked hard at the ball and aimed another mighty blow at it.

The ball shot straight up into the air.

'Did you see it?' shouted Dougal.

'It's gone up,' said Brian.

They looked. The ball was still rising. As they watched, it started to descend towards the flag where Uncle Hamish and Angus were looking at their ball.

'Oh, dear,' said Brian.

The ball come down, down, down, landed on the green, hit Uncle Hamish's ball and dropped into the hole.

'You've done it now,' said Brian, happily.

They walked slowly up to the green where Uncle Hamish and Angus were waiting.

'Er . . . sorry,' said Dougal.

'Ye should be,' said Uncle Hammish. 'But it was a bonny shot all the same. Did ye use the niblick?'

'Er . . . something like that,' said Dougal, nervously.

'Huh!' said Angus, loudly.

'Huh!' said Brian, quietly.

'Well, we'll see how ye fare on the next,' said Uncle Hamish. 'Come away.'

He went to the next patch.

On the tee Uncle Hamish was warming up, swinging a club.

'A long hole, this,' he said. 'My favourite.'

'Er . . . where *is* the hole?' said Dougal.

Uncle Hamish pointed. Away in the distance, just visible, fluttered a little flag.

'525 yards,' said Angus.

'Is there a bus?' said Brian.

'Shall I show the way?' said Uncle Hamish to Dougal.

'Please do,' said Dougal.

'Driver,' said Uncle Hamish, and Angus gave him a club. He hit the ball. It went a long way straight towards the flag.

'That'll do,' he said.

Dougal stepped up to the tee.

'Driver,' he said, and Brian handed him a club.

'Is that right?' he hissed.

'How should I know?' hissed Dougal back.

He sat the ball on its peg, closed his eyes and hit. There was a sharp crack and the ball sped away towards the flag.

'That'll do,' said Dougal, nonchalantly.

They set off towards where the two balls were lying. Dougal's had gone a little way beyond Uncle Hamish's.

Uncle Hamish hit his ball a great thwack and again it went straight and true towards the flag.

'Your turn,' he said to Dougal.

Dougal turned to Brian.

'Spoon,' he said.

'Spoon?!' said Brian. 'That's never a spoon shot. Take your mashie-tattie . . . '

And he giggled like anything.

'Have you gone quite off your head?' said Dougal. 'GIE ME YON SPOON!!'

Uncle Hamish nodded approvingly, and Brian handed Dougal a club.

Dougal stood over the ball, hoping his luck would hold.

He aimed and swung.

The ball stayed where it was, but the club went sideways like a bullet, hit a tree with a sharp crack, bounced straight up in the air, came down again, hit a stone, shot back towards Dougal and landed at his feet.

He laughed nervously.

'Just practising,' he said.

'Oh, aye?' said Uncle Hamish.

Dougal hit the ball quickly. It went along the ground like a rabbit and ended up just beside Uncle Hamish's.

'Oh, aye,' said Uncle Hamish.

'We'll be late for tea if we're not careful,' said Angus.

'We'll finish this hole,' said Uncle Hamish, and he strode away.

'A word of warning,' said Angus.

'Yes?' said Dougal.

'Don't beat him,' said Angus, 'or there'll be trouble.'

'What sort of trouble?' said Brian.

'Terrible trouble,' said Angus.

Uncle Hamish was looking at his ball.

'That's two shots to me and two shots to you,' he said to Dougal.

'Does that mean we're winning?' said Brian.

'It does not,' said Uncle Hamish.

He gave his ball a little hit and it rolled up very close to the hole and stopped.

He went over and tapped it in.

'Four,' he said. 'Ye need that to win.'

'I need what to win?' said Dougal.

'Ye need to put that ball in that hole in one more stroke and ye win,' said Uncle Hamish, and from the look on his face he didn't think it was very likely to happen.

Dougal took a club out of the bag without looking, went up to the ball and hit it.

It went sideways, hit Angus on a horn, bounced

on Brian's shell, over Uncle Hamish's foot and into the hole.

'Oh, lawks!' whispered Brian.

'Come, Angus,' said Uncle Hamish, slowly. 'We'll away.'

When they got back, Florence was pouring tea.

'Well, what have you two been doing?' she asked, brightly.

'We've been cleeking the mashies with a brassie baffy . . . and that,' said Brian. 'I enjoyed it.'

And he and Dougal started to giggle like anything.

'Tea, Dougal,' said Florence, sternly.

'May I have a spoon?' said Dougal, screeching with laughter.

'Try a niblick,' said Brian, shrieking and wiping his eyes on the cloth.

Uncle Hamish came in. They stopped laughing very quickly.

'And what have you been doing, Uncle Hamish?' said Florence.

Uncle Hamish looked at Dougal and Brian.

'I'd rather not talk about it,' he said, 'in the present company.'

# Highland Games

'Don't you think we've been here rather a long time?' said Florence, one day when they were all out for a walk. 'I don't want us to outstay our welcome.'

Everyone agreed that perhaps they should think of going back soon.

'We'll tell Uncle Hamish,' said Florence.

They told Uncle Hamish when they got back for lunch. He behaved rather strangely at the news. He got up and walked about, sniffed and sat down again.

'Ah, weel,' he said. 'Aye, aye, weel.'

Then he got up again and left without saying any more.

'Are all your relations like that?' said Brian.

'That's nothing,' said Dougal. 'You should see my Auntie Megsie; she goes very funny sometimes.'

'We must get him a present,' said Florence, thoughtfully.

'Yes,' said Ermintrude. 'Very important. He's been *sweet*.'

'But *what*?' said Mr Rusty.

They thought. Everything went quiet for a very long time.

Mr MacHenry coughed.

'Yes?' they said.

'I was just coughing,' said Mr MacHenry. 'Oh,' they said.

They thought some more.

'You know what I think,' said Brian, suddenly.

'Yes, we do,' said Dougal.

'No, don't be rotten,' said Brian.

'Tell us, Brian,' said Florence.

'Well, I think he'd like us to feel that we appreciated Scotland, so I think we should give him a Highland Games.'

He looked round brightly.

'Do you know,' said Dougal, 'I think you may finally have had an idea.'

'Yes,' said Florence, 'he'd like that. We'll do him some Highland Games as a farewell present.'

So it was decided, and of course it was to be kept a secret from Uncle Hamish.

'Er . . . there's just one little thing,' said Mr Rusty.

'Yes?' they said.

'Er . . . what *are* Highland Games?' he asked.

They all looked at Brian.

'Well, they're . . . er . . . games,' he said, 'and they're played in the . . . er . . . Highlands.'

'What sort of games?' said Mr Rusty.

'Oh, all sorts,' said Brian.

'You are being vague and devious, snail,' said Dougal.

Ermintrude had a suggestion; they would ask Angus.

Angus was asked.

'Is it the Games ye're planning?' he said. 'The *Games*?'

'Yes, the Games,' they said.

'Oh, aye, I ken weel the Games,' said Angus.

'Perhaps you'd be kind enough to explain them to us?' they said.

'Weel, 'tis a gathering,' said Angus. 'A *gathering* of athletic souls in brawny bodies . . . aye . . . that it is.'

'Could you explain a little more, Angus?' said Florence. 'What do they do?'

'Weel, they toss the caber,' said Angus, 'and they pitch the hammer and they bend the bawbee and they slither the shovel and they call the yowes to the knowes sometimes . . . if they've a mind.'

He paused reflectively.

'I was good at that,' he said.

'I shall toss the caber,' said Dougal. 'If I can find one.'

'I shall dance my Highland Fling,' said Florence. 'If I can learn it.'

'I shall play the bagpipes,' said Dylan. 'If I can borrow some.'

Mr MacHenry said he would provide floral tributes and decorations and Mr Rusty said he would announce the events.

'And I shall do a sword-dance,' said Ermintrude. 'If I can find some swords.'

'What about you?' said Dougal to Brian.

'I shall provide a surprise item,' said Brian.

'It would surprise me if you could *spell* item,' said Dougal.

'You may mock,' said Brian, 'but just you wait.'

The next few days were spent preparing. Dougal asked Big John to provide him with a caber and Big John said he couldn't get one before the day of the Games.

'Don't worry,' said Dougal, loftily. 'I don't need practice.'

The day of the Games arrived. After breakfast Uncle

Hamish was led out to the chosen field and seated in a special chair covered with flowers and bunting. All his attempts to discover what was happening were 'shushed' and he was given a cup of tea and told to 'wait and see'.

Dylan came out on to the field, called unnecessarily for silence and proceeded to open the games by playing so powerfully on the bagpipes that Uncle Hamish was seen to wilt.

Florence was next. Mr Rusty laid down boards flat, Dylan played the pipes and Florence gave Uncle Hamish her Highland Fling.

At the end Uncle Hamish roared to Florence that it was well done and would she come and sit by him?

Florence did so.

'What's next?' said Uncle Hamish, and Mr Rusty announced Ermintrude.

'Sword-dance,' whispered Florence.

'Oh, aye?' whispered Uncle Hamish.

Ermintrude hadn't been able to find any swords, so she laid a toasting fork and an old golf club on the dancing board Florence had used.

'Sword-dance,' she said proudly, stepping on and dis-appearing.

'Where's she gone?' said Uncle Hamish.

'I think the board broke,' said Florence, faintly. 'It must have been over a hole.'

Ermintrude's head appeared.

'Who put this board over a hole?' she said.

Mr Rusty confessed.

'It seemed a good idea at the time,' he said. 'In case anyone fell in.'

'Someone *did*,' said Ermintrude, 'but  the show must

go on.' And she performed her sword-dance to great acclaim – especially from Angus.

Mr Rusty announced Dougal.

'Caber tossing,' whispered Florence.

'Oh, aye?' whispered Uncle Hamish.

Dougal stepped into the middle of the arena.

'Big John,' he called. 'I'll trouble you for the caber.'

Big John ambled on pulling after him a tree-trunk of prodigious length and girth.

Dougal paled.

'What's that?' he asked.

'That's your caber,' said Big John.

'That's not a caber,' said Dougal, 'that's a *tree*.'

'A *small* tree,' said Big John, 'called a caber. You pick it up and throw it.'

'Pick it up and throw it?!' said Dougal, aghast.

'That's the general idea,' said Big John.

'I'm not sure the RSPCA would let me,' said Dougal.

He looked round. The Games field was full of expectant faces.

'I must be mad,' he groaned, and he got his shoulders under the caber and started to heave.

'Careful, Dougal!' called Florence.

'Now she tells me,' gritted Dougal, doing little runs backwards and forwards with the caber pointing straight up.

'Right, you've got it!' shouted Brian. 'Toss it forward.'

Dougal tried. The caber tilted. Everyone gasped. The caber tilted more and Dougal set off at a run down the field.

'Throw it,' they shouted.

'I can't,' screeched Dougal.

'Let go,' they shouted.

'I can't!' screamed Dougal. 'It's caught in me kilt!'

He was gathering more speed, and as they watched he finally disappeared with a last little wail through a hole in the wall at the end of the field.

'He'll likely end up in Fife,' said Uncle Hamish.

There was a faint crash from the distance, and with a loud squawk Dougal flew back over into the field and landed in the middle with a bump.

'Are you all right, Dougal?' called Florence, anxiously.

Dougal got up and put his kilt straight.

'I have just,' he said slowly, 'run fourteen miles holding a tree. I have hit a rock and been flung back like a dob of mud into the middle of a field. OF COURSE I AM NOT ALL RIGHT!!'

'I don't think you got the principle of the thing quite right, old mate,' said Brian.

Dougal turned slowly and advanced on him.

'Why are you advancing on me like that?' said Brian, nervously.

'Because I am going to bury your head in the mud and laugh a lot,' said Dougal.

'But it's time for my surprise,' said Brian.

'Time for Brian's surprise!' they all shouted.

'Mollusc,' said Dougal, 'this had better be good.'

Mr Rusty called for silence. Brian went to the middle of the field, bowed right, left and centre and let out a piercing whistle.

There was a rushing of wings and hundreds of pigeons flew low over the field, circled and went high into the sky. With a bang a hole opened in the field and thousands of balloons floated up. The pigeons swooped down, caught the balloons and swooped up again high into the air. They let them go against the blue sky and the balloons danced together.

The air filled with the sound of a thousand pipers playing Uncle Hamish's favourite tunes and with a PING and a BONG a table appeared covered with a huge tea, with a vast cake in the shape of a letter H.

'Brian!' breathed Florence. 'What a surprise. How *did* you do it?'

Brian smiled modestly.

'I had a little help,' he said, and there was Zebedee bonging around the middle of the field laughing like anything.

'Zebedee, of course,' said Florence.

Uncle Hamish was very moved.

'It's been a great day,' he said, 'and it's been great having ye here. Ye must come again.'

'Aye, haste ye back,' said Angus.

'We will,' they said.

The next morning after they'd all packed and had a last look round, the train was found fast asleep in a siding and everyone loaded in.

'Oh, are we going back already?' said the train, yawning.

Florence looked at the hills and the trees.

'It's time to go,' she said, sadly.

Uncle Hamish and Angus and Big John packed provisions into the train and stood on the platform to wave goodbye.

'I may cry,' said Brian.

'Don't be so soft,' said Dougal, sniffing.

Uncle Hamish blew up his bagpipes and started to play a long sad tune.

'I *shall* cry,' said Brian.

'Got a hanky?' said Dougal.

'There's always next year,' said Zebedee, and the train gave a little toot.

They all brightened.

'It's April in the garden,' said Mr MacHenry, thoughtfully.

It was time to go.

So they went.

PART 3

# Dougal round the world



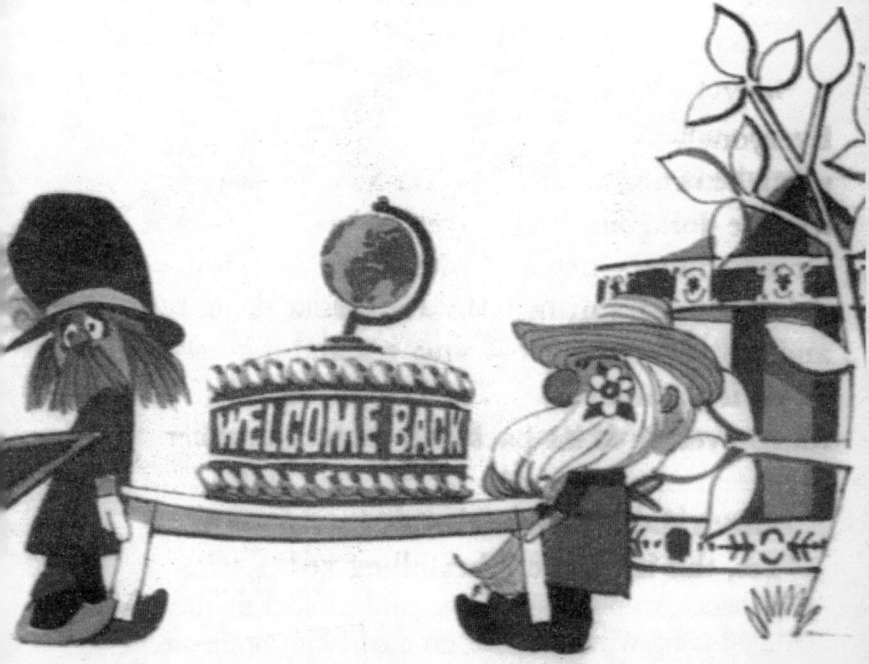

# The start

Everyone was sitting in Zebedee's garden. It was a beautiful warm day and no one really felt like doing anything except what they were already doing – sitting in Zebedee's garden. Zebedee wasn't sitting. He was springing in and out of his kitchen serving tea and sandwiches and rock cakes. Dougal sighed, rolled over on his back and nibbled another cake.

'This is the life,' he said.

'Yes, this is the life,' they all agreed.

Zebedee stopped springing and looked at them all – Dougal lying with his head on a cushion, Brian stretched

out on a rug. Dylan fast asleep. Mr Rusty and Mr MacHenry nodding off, and Florence lying with her head resting on Ermintrude.

'More tea anyone?' he said.

Everyone stirred a little.

'I might force down another cup,' said Dougal, lazily.

'And I could toy with another radish butty,' said Brian.

No one else spoke. Zebedee suddenly could stand it no longer.

'WAKE UP!' he shouted.

'ALL WAKE UP!!'

Everyone woke up, wondering what on earth was the matter.

'What's the matter, Zebedee? said Florence.

'*You're* the matter,' said Zebedee, 'all
of you. Look at you, lying around doing
nothing. I can't understand why you're all just lying
here! You've all got very lazy lately and I'm *very*
worried about you.'

'Well, what do you want us to do?' said Florence.

'I'm not sure,' said Zebedee, 'but I know you ought to
be doing *something*.'

'Would you like me to do a dance?' said Brian,
giggling at Dougal.

Dougal giggled back.

'Now you're not being serious,' said Zebedee. 'Listen.'

Everyone put on a serious face and listened.

'I've been thinking,' said Zebedee, 'and I think the
time has come for me to take you all in hand. You stay

in this garden all day and every day and you never *see* anything else. Your minds will wither – you need to broaden your horizons – you need to get out and about.'

'Perhaps we should go round the world,' said Dougal, 'on a bicycle built for seven.'

Everyone laughed like anything.

'Or we could run,' squeaked Brian. 'Shouldn't take more than fifteen years.'

Everyone shrieked with laughter again.

'Perhaps there's a bus,' said Ermintrude.

This made them laugh even more, and they all rolled about wiping their eyes and choking with mirth.

But Zebedee was looking very thoughtful.

'Um . . .' he said, 'I wonder.'

Gradually they all stopped laughing and looked at Zebedee.

Zebedee looked more thoughtful than ever.

'He's looking at bit thoughtful,' whispered Brian.

Suddenly Zebedee seemed to come to a decision.

'Right,' he said, briskly. 'You've given me an idea. Travel, that's the answer. I don't suppose any of you have ever been *anywhere* or seen *anything*.'

'I've been to London,' said Ermintrude. 'Smithfield. It was great fun.'

'Did you get a prize?' said Florence.

'I'd rather not talk about *that*,' said Ermintrude, darkly.

'Well, I've been to London too,' said Dougal. 'Crufts.'

'Did you get a prize, old pedigree?' said Brian.

'I'd rather not talk about it either,' said Dougal. 'Suffice it to say there was *hanky-panky*.'

Florence was a bit worried. She could see Zebedee was serious.

'Er . . . if we are going to travel,' she asked, 'where are we going?'

'Everywhere,' said Zebedee. 'I'm taking you round the world.'

There was a stunned silence.

'Round the world!' breathed Florence.

'Round the world!' said Dougal.

'Which world does he mean?' said Brian.

'There's only one, you great oaf,' said Dougal. 'You're standing on it.'

'Eek!' said Brian, jumping on to the rug.

Mr MacHenry and Mr Rusty thought they were perhaps a bit old for world travel and they decided to go to Bournemouth instead.

'A spot of sea air,' said Mr Rusty.

'Do us a power of good,' said Mr MacHenry.

So Zebedee agreed that Mr Rusty and Mr MacHenry could go to Bournemouth, but the others were definitely going round the world.

'Willy-nilly?' said Brian.

'Willy-nilly!' said Zebedee.

'Who's this Willy?' said Dougal, furiously.

'No one you know,' said Brian.

Zebedee asked if they were all ready because he was going to start before anything happened to change things.

'I'll take you to Paris first,' he said. 'That's a good place to start round the world from.'

'I can't see it makes much difference,' muttered Dougal.

'Ready?' said Zebedee. 'Close your eyes.'

'Ready,' they all said closing them, and with a magic 'whoosh' they were off, leaving Mr MacHenry and Mr Rusty looking up the train times for Bournemouth . . .

'You can open your eyes now,' said Zebedee a little later on.

They did so.

'Gracious,' said Florence.

They were all standing on top of a huge tower and all around them, far below, was the city of Paris.

'Paris,' said Zebedee, proudly.

'What's this we're standing on?' said Brian.

'The Eiffel Tower,' said Zebedee. 'I chose this because it's high – good for launching.'

'LAUNCHING?!' said Dougal, faintly. 'Launching what?'

'Well, it so happens I have access to a magic carpet,' said Zebedee, 'and you can't beat a magic carpet for actual travel.'

'You don't think we'd do better by BOAC?' said Dougal.

'No, I don't,' said Zebedee. 'Now listen carefully.'

They all listened carefully.

'I have given the instructions,' said Zebedee, 'and I want you all to meet me back in the garden and tell me where you've been. But right round the world, mind – no skipping back when I'm not looking. Right round, mind. Good-bye.'

And with a springing noise he was gone, leaving them all standing on top of the Eiffel Tower feeling a little lost.

'Do you think I've got time to buy a new hat?' said Ermintrude. 'I don't get to Paris often.'

'You're not the only one,' said Dougal.

'May I ask a question?' said Brian.

'No, you may not,' said Dougal.

'Yes, of course you may,' said Florence.

'Oh, once he starts he'll never stop,' said Dougal.

'It's a very *basic* question,' said Brian. 'I just wanted to know where the carpet was.'

Everyone was astounded. No one else had thought of it. Zebedee had gone on and on about the carpet, but no one had thought to ask where it was or how they found it.

'Look,' said Dougal. 'I expect it's all a big joke. Let's go down, get some tea and catch a bus home.'

'No, I don't think it was a joke,' said Florence, slowly. 'Zebedee's not like that.'

She gazed out across the city, shading her eyes with her hand.

'Oo, I think I see something,' she said.

They all looked. Coming towards them was a flat object. It got nearer and nearer, did a zooming turn over the the tower and landed just beside them.

It was a carpet, and sitting on it was a little man in a turban and a long robe.

'Afternoon all,' he said, in a broad Lancashire accent. 'You'll be the party then.'

They agreed they probably were the party.

'Thought you might be,' said the man. 'I was told Eiffel Tower. Sorry I'm a bit late, but the thermals were reet tricky over Baghdad. Get on.'

They looked at the carpet doubtfully.

'Is there room for all of us, dear driver?' said Ermintrude.

'The name's Grimbly,' said the little man. 'Mustapha Grimbly, but you can call me George if you've a mind. Ever been on a carpet before?'

They said they hadn't and was it safe?

'Safe as houses,' said George, 'and the best way to travel in the world. I was on the buses before this job. Buses are all right, but you can't beat a carpet.'

He gave a loud laugh.

'Ee . . . that's a good one,' he said, wheezing. 'Can't beat a carpet! Ho! Ho! Ho! What about that?!'

'What about what?' said Dougal.

George looked at him.

'Can't beat a carpet. Don't you get it? Carpet? Beating? Oh, never mind – get on.'

He started to laugh again, muttering 'Can't beat a carpet' to himself.

'We've got a right one here,' whispered Dougal.

They all got on. Although the carpet *seemed* to be quite small there was plenty of room for everyone. George sat at the front, Dougal, Brian and Florence in the middle, and Dylan and Ermintrude at the back.

'Ready?' said George.

'Ready,' they said, a little nervously.

'Right then, we'll be off,' said George, and the carpet rose slowly into the air and set off through the sky across Paris. George took them on a little circular tour so they could have a look round. They saw the churches and the bridges and the river and the stations and the parks.

'No one seems to be taking much notice,' said Florence, looking down.

'It's because we're British,' said Dougal. 'They're like that, the French.'

'Oh,' said Florence.

They flew on over Paris and south across France. It was beautifully warm with just a little breeze and the carpet made no noise at all.

Suddenly Brian gave a great 'whoop!' and started to roar with laughter.

The others looked at him in surprise.

'What's your problem, mollusc?' said Dougal, coldly.

'Can't beat a carpet!' wheezed Brian. 'Oh, that's very good. Hee! Hee! Can't beat a carpet! Ho! Ho! Hee! Hee!'

Dougal sighed.

'What *has* the world done to deserve *him*?' he muttered, and they sped on southwards through the evening sky.

# *Italy*

Everyone was asleep when George landed the carpet on their first stop round the world. The slight bump as they hit the ground woke them up and they all looked around. They were in a beautiful open square. A fountain was splashing and gurgling in the middle and all round there were little cafés with tables and chairs set under big umbellas.

'Italy,' said George, briefly.

'Oh, I thought Italy was bigger than this,' said Brian.

'Really!' said Dougal. 'Really! This isn't all of it, you great clump. It's twice as big as this *easily*!'

'Where exactly are we, George?' said Florence.

'Florence,' said George.

'Yes?' said Florence.

'What *are* you two on about?' said Dougal.

'I'm not sure,' said Florence. 'I was just asking George whereabouts in Italy we were.'

'And I told you,' said George. 'Florence.'

'Yes,' said Florence.

'Yes,' said George, and he began to hoot with laughter.

'Oh dear, he's off again.' whispered Dougal.

'I think he means we're . . . like . . . in the *town* of Florence, mam,' said Dylan.

'Oh,' said Florence. 'He means *Florence*.'

George laughed some more and wiped his eyes.

'Sorry,' he said, 'I never could resist a good jest. Funny, wasn't it?'

'Absolutely hilarious,' said Dougal not laughing at all, but Florence and the others agreed it was a very good joke.

'And I've always wanted to see the Leaning Tower of Florence,' said Brian, happily.

'Oh, you poor befuddled mollusc,' said Dougal, 'don't you know *anything*?'

'Not a lot,' said Brian happily, 'but what I do know is very gem-like.'

Dougal groaned.

'Tell him where the Leaning Tower is,' he said to Florence.

'No, *you* tell him,' said Florence, somewhat pointedly.

'Well,' said Dougal, 'it's in . . . it's in . . . um . . . Oh, let him find out for himself.'

'Pisa,' said Ermintrude, suddenly.

'I beg your pardon?' said Dougal.

'Pisa,' said Emintrude. 'That's where the Leaning Tower is. I remember it from school.'

'Well, I want to see it,' said Brian.

George assured him that they would go and see the Leaning Tower, but first they should all have some breakfast.

'That's the first sensible thing anyone's said for *ages*,' said Dougal, and he led the way across the square to one of the little cafés.

'That was a good joke about Florence, wasn't it?' said Brian, chattily.

'Oh, be quiet,' said Dougal.

After breakfast they wandered round the city and saw all the sights. Ermintrude bought some earrings, Dylan bought a guitar.

'Oh´ dear,' whispered Dougal, 'now I suppose it's going to be *Tosca* all the way!'

'No,' said Dylan, who had heard, 'but I shall sing to the people and bring . . . like . . . happiness into their lives.'

'That's what I was afraid of,' said Dougal, sighing.

'Well, at least he's not asleep,' said Brian.

'You're going to wish he was in a minute,' said Dougal.

Dylan wandered into the middle of a little square and started to play. He was immediately surrounded by dozens of very small children who followed him clapping their hands to the rhythm.

'Rome, Rome for a change,' Dylan sang, and disappeared round a corner surrounded by children.

'There goes the Pied Rabbit of Florence,' giggled Dougal.

George came along and told them they ought to be going if they wanted to see the Leaning Tower before it got dark.

'I'm afraid Dylan's wandered off,' said Florence.

George sighed.

'Aye, someone always wanders off,' he said. 'Never mind. Get on and we'll find him.'

They all got on the carpet and floated over the city looking for Dylan. He wasn't hard to find. He was walking along a wide street followed by about two hundred children all singing at the tops of their voices.

Everyone called to Dylan, but he didn't hear. George swooped low and they shouted again, but still Dylan wandered on, playing and singing.

'I expect he's dropped off,' said Dougal.

'But he's singing,' said Brian.

'That wouldn't stop him sleeping,' said Dougal. 'Not that rabbit.'

George swooped low again and just touched the tips of Dylan's ears. Dylan stopped and looked up.

'Come on!' said Dougal. 'We' ve got to get to Pisa!'

Dylan climbed on to a low wall, George banked the carpet, flew close to Dylan and the others pulled him on board.

'Like . . . good-bye, kids!' he shouted, and the children waved and waved until they were just little tiny specks in the far distance.

'Crazy!' said Dylan. 'Really crazy,' and he put down his guitar, curled up and went to sleep.

He was still asleep when they got to Pisa, so they left him while they went to look at the Leaning Tower. George stayed behind too to have a little doze.

The Tower was a marvellous sight, a huge building tilted over at an angle.

'One of the Seven Wonders of the World,' breathed Florence.

'Why is it one of the Seven Wonders?' said Brian.

'Because it's a wonder it doesn't fall over,' said Dougal. 'Anyone can see that.'

'Well, I don't fall over when I lean,' said Brian, 'so am I a wonder?'

And he stood by the Tower and leaned as far as he could.

He fell over.

Dougal screeched with laughter.

'You potty little ploppet!' he said. 'Won't you *ever* learn?'

'I hope not,' said Brian.

Ermintrude walked all the way round the Tower.

'It really is *marvellous*,' she sighed. 'The things you *see* when you travel.'

She yawned and leaned against the Tower.

It creaked.

'Oh, I feel quite sleepy,' she said, leaning a bit harder. 'I shall have to sit down in a minute.'

The Tower creaked again.

'Er . . . Ermintrude . . .' said Florence, 'I shouldn't . . .'

But Ermintrude had closed her eyes and had fallen asleep leaning against the Tower. As she slept she leaned harder and harder, and gradually the Tower got more and more upright.

'Er . . . Ermintrude,' said Florence anxiously, 'please wake up.'

The Tower slid a little more. Ermintrude gave a little snore. Suddenly the Tower snapped completely upright, and Ermintrude slid down and fell over with a bump.

She woke up.

'Oh! It's all right!' she said. 'I was just dozing.'

The others looked at the Tower in horror.

'Ooh, you've done it now,' said Dougal.

'Done what, dear dog?' said Ermintrude.

'You've straightened the Leaning Tower,' said Florence.

Ermintrude laughed.

'Silly girl,' she said, 'what *do* you mean?'

She turned and looked at the Tower, gave a little 'moo' and fell over in a dead faint.

It was a very difficult moment. Florence flapped her handkerchief at Ermintrude to try to bring her round, Dougal rushed about in little circles and Brian just sat on the ground and laughed.

'What are we going to *do*?' said Dougal, in a frenzy.

'Try pushing it back,' said Brian, giggling.

Florence flapped her handkerchief harder and Ermintrude gradually came to.

'Where am I?' she said, faintly.

'You're very close to the Upright Tower of Pisa,' said Brian.

Ermintrude looked and fainted away again.

'Oh dear, oh dear,' said Florence, 'this really won't do at all. Dougal! Do something!'

'I *am* doing something,' said Dougal. 'I'm circling and *thinking*.'

Florence fanned away at Ermintrude.

'If we could wake her up she might be able to push it over again,' she said.

'We're in a lot of trouble if she can't,' said Dougal. 'People come here to see a Leaning Tower, not an ordinary old upright one.'

'I've got an idea,' said Brian, suddenly.

'Yes?' said Florence.

'Why don't we dig the ground away on one side,' said Brian, 'and then when people stand there one leg will be higher than the other and they'll *lean*.'

'Yes?' said Florence.

'Well, if they lean the Tower will appear to lean also,' said Brian, triumphantly.

Dougal stopped circling and looked at Brian.

'Brilliant,' he said. 'Absolutely brilliant. All we need is a couple of bulldozers and about three years' hard labour. Great oaf!'

'It was just a thought,' said Brian.

'Well, *stop* thinking if that's the best you can do,' said Dougal.

Suddenly they heard voices.

'Someone's coming,' hissed Dougal. 'Quick! Hide!'

There was nowhere to hide so they all crouched down behind Ermintrude.

The voices got nearer. It was two ladies carrying cameras and talking to each other rather loudly.

'You know I'm sure we should have had a guide, Pauline,' said one.

'Oh, Alice,' said the other, 'what do you want a guide for? The Leaning Tower is the Leaning Tower.'

'Oh, what a quaint old seat,' they said, sitting on Ermintrude and looking at the Tower.

There was silence for a moment.

'Does that Tower appear to be leaning to you, Pauline?' said Alice.

'No, Alice, it does not,' said Pauline.

Ermintrude gave a little tiny moo.

'She's waking up!' hissed Brian.

'Well, tell her to stop!' hissed Dougal.

'Stop!' shouted Brian, very loud.

The two ladies jumped into the air.

'I told you we should have had a guide, Pauline,' said Alice nervously, and they both hurried away without looking round.

Ermintrude groaned and stirred. Florence fanned her

again and she got up very slowly.

'Thank you, dear heart,' she said. 'Sorry to be a nuisance, but I was quite overcome with shame.'

She looked at the Tower.

'What *have* I done?' she moaned.

'Do you think you could give it a little push back?' said Florence. 'I think it would be best if you could.'

'Well, I'll try, dear, but I feel rather frail at the moment,' said Ermintrude, and she gave the Tower a little push.

It didn't move.

'Try harder,' said Florence.

Ermintrude tried harder. The Tower creaked a little and started to move.

'You're doing it!' shouted Brian. 'Just a bit more!'

Ermintrude pushed a little more. The Tower moved a little more, then a little more and then it started to tilt quite fast.

'You can stop now!' shouted Brian.

'I stopped ages ago,' said Ermintrude.

'Oh lawks!' said Brian.

Dougal hurtled round to the other side of the Tower and tried to hold it.

'Come and help!' he screeched.

The Tower tilted dangerously.

'Put a stone under it!' shouted Brian.

'I'll put you under it,' screeched Dougal, but he did manage to push a stone under the bottom of the Tower.

The Tower gradually stopped.

They stepped back.

'Phew!' said Dougal. 'That was close.'

They looked at the Tower. It was leaning rather more

than before. In fact it was leaning a *lot* more than before.

'Do you think anyone will notice?' said Florence, anxiously. 'It's not quite the same as it was.'

'Oh, a leaning tower is a leaning tower,' said Brian. 'I think we did very well.'

'What do you mean, "we"?' said Dougal, panting.

'Well, I encouraged by my presence and my cool thinking,' said Brian. 'They also serve who only stand and watch, you know.'

'And they also get thumped who only talk too much,' said Dougal, threateningly.

'Don't you dare!' said Brian. 'I'm littler than you.'

'Now stop that, you two,' said Florence.

'I'm sorry to have been a nuisance,' said Ermintrude.

'That's all right,' said Florence.

They went back to the carpet. George was busy making sandwiches and opening bottles of milk.

'Seen enough?' he asked.

'For a lifetime,' said Dougal, with feeling.

They all had something to eat. Dylan woke up and joined them.

'Have I got . . . like . . . time for a quick peep at the Tower?' he said.

'If you're very quick,' said George, and Dylan went to have a look while the others cleared up.

'That's the craziest thing,' said Dylan when he came back.

'How does it ever stay leaning like that without falling over?'

'It's got a stone under it,' said Brian.

'And I hope no one ever moves it,' muttered Dougal.

'Right, ready to go?' asked George.

Everyone got on the carpet.

'Where are we going now?' asked Florence.

'You're all going to sleep,' said George, 'and when you wake up you'll see. Reet?'

'Reet,' they said, and they floated up over Pisa, did a turn round the Tower with George looking at it in rather a puzzled way, and headed south again through the warm evening air.

# *Morocco*

Everyone was asleep when they landed again. The little bump woke them up, and they all yawned and stretched and looked around. George had brought the carpet down close to a little clump of palm-trees and all around as far as the eye could see there was nothing but sand.

'I think the tide's out,' said Brian, brightly. 'Must be Clacton.'

'Oh, don't be such a great oaf,' said Dougal. 'It's nothing like Clacton.'

'Have you ever been to Clacton?' said Brian.

'That's beside the point,' said Dougal.

'No, it's beside the *sea*,' said Brian.

Florence told them to stop arguing and asked George if there was anywhere close they could go for breakfast.

'All taken care of,' said George. 'All part of the service,' and he gave a piercing whistle. A large clump of dates dropped out of the palm-tree, landed on Dougal's head and finished up in the centre of the carpet.

George looked up.

'Funny,' he said, 'that's never happened before. Anyway, try some of those to be going on with,' and he gave another very loud whistle.

Dougal winced.

'I hope he doesn't do that often,' he said. 'I've got very sensitive ears.'

Ermintrude was munching a date.

'Ooh, delicious,' she said. 'Do try some.'

They all tried some and admitted they were indeed very delicious.

'There's nothing like a date fresh from the palm,' sighed Ermintrude.

'And there's nothing like tea fresh from the pot,' said Dougal, 'but I suppose I shall have to wait till I get home for *that*.'

He was wrong. A small cloud of dust appeared on the horizon. Something was coming towards them very fast. It got nearer and nearer and finally stopped. The dust settled slowly and there was a camel with a basket hanging on either side of its hump.

'Sorry to be late, George,' it said. 'Terrible crowd in Marrakesh.'

'That's all right, Sandy,' said George, 'we've only been here a minute.'

He went across to the camel and started to get things out of the baskets. There was a table-cloth, knives, forks and spoons, teacups and saucers, plates and bowls, a large pot of tea, milk and sugar, lettuce and cucumber, cornflakes and boiled eggs.

'Well!' said Ermintrude. 'We can hardly complain about the service.'

'No, we certainly can't,' said Florence, happily. 'I like going round the world.'

They all had breakfast and when they had finished George packed the things back in the baskets.

'What's the plan then, Sandy?' he asked.

The camel munched a date thoughtfully.

'Well,' he said, 'I thought they'd like a quick saunter around the market now, flip over the Atlas Mountains for a cup of coffee, drop in at Casablanca for lunch, tea at Joe's Oasis Caff and early bed in Fez. What do you think?

He got up and sauntered over to Ermintrude.

'How about you and me taking a quick look at the Casbah?' he said, with a huge wink.

'Cheeky thing,' said Ermintrude, giggling.

'Don't take any notice of him, miss,' said George, 'he's quite harmless.'

Ermintrude looked a little disappointed, the camel munched another date, gave another big wink and went back to George.

'Well?' he said.

'Fine,' said George, 'we'll do what you say, Carpet or train?'

'What *are* they talking about?' hissed Dougal. 'How do we get a train out here?'

'I think they probably know what they're talking about,' said Florence, but she did see Dougal's point – there didn't seem much chance of catching a train from where they were. There wasn't even a station.

But George let out another of his piercing whistles and in the distance another cloud of dust appeared.

'Train's coming,' said George, briefly.

'Good-bye, all,' said Sandy, and he trotted away just as the other cloud of dust arrived.

It was six camels.

'All aboard,' said George, and he folded the carpet neatly, asked the first camel to kneel down and threw the carpet across its neck.

'All aboard,' he said again.

'This is a *train*?' said Dylan.

'Camel train,' said George. 'Hurry up.' The camels all knelt down and waited. 'Which bit do you sit on?' whispered Florence.

'Don't ask me,' whispered Dougal.

They watched George as he got on his camel. He gave a little jump and sat on top of the hump.

'Come on,' he said, 'or we'll never get there.'

'I'm not sure we'll get there anyway,' muttered Dougal, but he got on a hump and perched there wobbling.

'Dougal of Arabia, I presume?' said Brian.

'I'll throw a clump of dates at you if you're not careful,' said Dougal. 'Just get on and be quiet.'

So Brian got on and so did Florence and Dylan. Ermintrude had a little difficulty.

'I think someone will have to give me a leg up,' she wailed.

George got off and went over to Ermintrude. He looked at her and he looked at the camel.

'Everybody come and help,' he said, 'this might be difficult.'

Everyone got off again and went over to help Ermintrude.

'Now when I say "push", push,' said George.

'PUSH!'

Everyone pushed. Ermintrude slithered up the side of the camel, teetered for a moment on the top and then slithered down the other side with a bump. They tried again. Erminrude went up again, teetered again and slid off again.

'Try holding on,' said Florence.

'What *with*, dear thing?' said Ermintrude.

They pushed again, and again she fell off.

Ermintrude was furious and became very determined.

'Stand aside!' she ordered, and strode off into the desert.

'Where's she going?' said Brian.

'I can't imagine,' said Dougal.

Ermintrude stopped about fifty yards away. She turned, lowered her head, gave a little moo, thundered towards the camel and leapt on.

'I'm on!' she cried. 'I'm on! Let's go! What are we all waiting for?!'

The others got back on and waited for George to start.

'Hold on,' he said. 'Here we go.'

The camels got up on to their back legs. Everyone slithered forward. Then the camels got on to their front legs. Everyone slithered back again.

Ermintrude fell off.

'Oh, this is the last straw!' she wailed.

The camel turned his head slowly.

'You may be right, madam,' he said, laconically.

This made Ermintrude more determined than ever. She rushed at the camel and leapt on again. This time she stayed on.

'Bravo!' everyone shouted, and they were off in a single file across the desert.

It was a very strange sight. George leading and singing 'She's a lassie from Lancashire'; Florence next, perched high on her camel and singing the choruses with George; then Dylan, fast asleep, having tied himself on with a rope; then Brian, who had retired into his shell and was looking rather like a hump on top of a hump;

then Dougal, who had slithered off the camel's back on to its neck and was clinging on grimly; and last Ermintrude, happily astride and giving an occasional moo of delight.

They approached a huge red wall. Behind it they could see towers and palm-trees, and they could hear a lot of noise.

George turned and shouted over his shoulder.

'Market!'

They went through a low gate in the wall and found themselves in a huge open square. It was crowded with people and very noisy. George led the way and finally stopped under some palm-trees by a little pool of water. The camels knelt down and everyone fell off except Dylan who was still tied on and still asleep.

Dougal looked at him.

'He'll set the record for round-the-world sleeping, that rabbit,' he said, untying the rope.

Dylan fell off.

'What? Like . . . er . . . what? he said. 'Where are we, man? Like . . . where?'

'It's Notting Hill Gate,' said Dougal, sarcastically.

'Oh,' said Dylan, and he rolled over and went back to sleep.

George gave the camels some dates and told them they'd be back soon.

'I expect you'd all like a little something?' he said to the others.

'I should love a little something,' said Brian. 'Is there an Arabian radish?'

'I shouldn't wonder,' said George. 'Come along, all.'

They started to go, but Florence noticed Ermintrude wasn't with them.

'Where's Ermintrude?' she said.

They looked. There was no sign of her.

'Perhaps she sneaked off for a hay sandwich,' said Dougal. 'Be just like her.'

'We'd better find her,' said Florence, anxiously.

'Aye, we'd better,' said George.

So they set out to look for Ermintrude.

They went through the market-place and looked amongst all the people. No Ermintrude. They asked a group of donkeys if they'd seen her, but they hadn't. They asked a tall Arab policeman, but he hadn't seen her either. They wandered in and out of the market stalls, past jugglers and fortune-tellers, past fruit-stands and sweet-stands, but there was no sign of Ermintrude anywhere.

Finally, they came to a café and all sat down, feeling rather tired. Brian and Florence ordered some orange juice and Dougal and George ordered some tea. The waiter brought it. The orange juice looked just like orange juice, but the tea was in a tall glass full of green leaves.

'What's this!?' said Dougal.

'That's tea,' said George.

'TEA!!' said Dougal. 'It looks like a glass of wet grass!!'

'It's mint tea,' said George. 'Very refreshing.'

Dougal looked at the glass of mint tea.

'Oh, to be in England,' he sighed, and took a sip.

It was very sweet and very good.

'Ooh!' he said, brightening. 'Not bad.'

'There you are, Dougal,' said Florence. 'You must always be prepared to try something *new*.'

'Want some?' said Dougal.

'No, thank you,' said Florence.

They gazed around. The square was full of colours and the sun was very hot. The only thing missing was Ermintrude.

Yoo! Hoo! Yoo! Hoo! they heard.

'That's Ermintrude!' said Florence.

Yoo! Hoo! Yoo! Hoo! they heard again, and Ermintrude appeared followed by a very small Arab in a very large robe.

She sat down.

She was wearing a veil over her face, a huge pair of bloomers covered in a violent flower design and had a large handbag hanging round her neck.

'I've been shopping,' she said, happily.

'We'd never have known,' said Dougal, giggling.

'What's that on your face?' said Brian, hanging on to his chair and laughing.

'It's my yashmak,' said Ermintrude, proudly. 'No lady wanders about *here* without one.'

Dougal and Brian clung on to each other, laughing like anything.

'Who's your friend?' they hooted, pointing to the small Arab in the robe.

'This is Mustapha,' said Ermintrude. 'He's been *very* helpful.'

Mustapha pointed at Ermintrude.

''Ow much?' he said.

George shook his head.

'Not for sale,' he said.

Mustapha looked surprised.

''Ow much?' he said again.

'Poor boy,' said Ermintrude, 'I think he wants to buy me.'

'How much will you give us!?' shouted Brian and Dougal, but Florence told them not to be silly.

'I'm afraid our friend is not for sale,' she said to Mustapha.

'Yours for four pence!!' screamed Dougal and Brian, purple with mirth.

'Now hush, you two!' said Florence, and she told

Ermintrude not to wander off by herself in future.

'Sorry, dear thing,' said Ermintrude. 'Good-bye, Mustapha dear!'

Mustapha bowed and started to go away. Then he came back and pointed at Brian.

''Ow much?' he said.

'Nothing!' shouted Dougal. 'Take him! A present!'

'Don't be rotten!' said Brian, clinging on to his chair and squeaking.

Mustapha bowed again, looked round and then wandered away.

'Nearly got rid of you that time!' said Dougal.

'Didn't want to buy *you* though, did he?' jeered Brian.

'Now once and for all stop it, you two,' said Florence, severely.

So Brian and Dougal stopped it and they all followed George back to the camels.

'I think we'll take the carpet now,' said George. 'Thanks, lads.'

They all thanked the camels for the ride across the desert. Then they woke Dylan up.

'Time to go,' they said.

'Already?' said Dylan, stretching. 'It's a great place this.'

'You know,' whispered Dougal, 'I think he may get round the world without seeing anything but the ground he's lying on.'

'Well, he's enjoying himself,' whispered Brian. 'That's the main thing.'

And that did seem to be the main thing as they got on the carpet, rose high over the market square and flew eastwards away from the setting sun.

# *India*

The first thing they noticed when they landed again was the heat. It was very hot even though it was early in the morning.

'Where are we?' said Florence.

'India,' said George. 'Great little place. I always like coming here.'

'Isn't this where all the tea comes from?' said Dougal, thoughtfully.

'A lot of it,' said George. 'Do you want some?'

Dougal said he would rather like some, so they all had breakfast brought on trays by Indians in very bright coloured turbans.

After breakfast they took a little walk. For some reason Ermintrude was a great favourite wherever they went. People hung flowers round her neck, great garlands of yellow and white and red. She looked very pretty.

'You look very pretty, Ermintrude,' said Florence.

'Thank you, dear,' said Ermintrude, as another string of flowers was added by yet another admirer.

'She won't be able to see soon,' whispered Dougal.

'She is a bit festooned,' whispered Brian.

They came to a large open square and stopped to look around.

'Want to see some snake-charmers?' asked George.

'Oo, yes please,' said Florence.

'Er . . . just a moment,' said Dougal. 'Did you say *snake*-charmers?'

'Yes,' said George. 'Snakes. Cobras, adders, things like that.'

'Actual *poisonous* snakes?' said Dougal.

'So they tell me,' said George. 'Don't you like them?'

'Oh no, it's not *that*,' said Dougal. 'I mean, some of my best friends . . . er . . . but . . .'

'Oh, come on, old charmer,' said Brian. 'Let's go and have a look.'

'I'm *coming*,' said Dougal. 'Don't rush me!'

They went into the middle of the square. Sitting on the ground was an old man in a loin-cloth and a turban. He had a pipe-like instrument in his hands and a basket at his feet. George greeted him and whispered something in his ear.

The man nodded, gave a little cough and started to play the pipe. The music was very weird.

'Oh, that's beautiful,' said Dylan, closing his eyes. '*Beautiful*,' and he sat down and nodded off to sleep.

The music continued.

'Where are the snakes?' hissed Dougal.

'Is that one behind you?' said Brian.

Dougal gave a screech and leapt three feet into the air.

'Oh no, sorry,' said Brian, 'it's just a twig.'

'Oo!! One of these days . . . ! !' said Dougal, threateningly.

'Sh!!' said Florence. 'Something's happening.'

Something was.

Out in the basket came a cobra, waving and weaving

to and fro. The music got louder and faster, and more and more of the cobra appeared. Its hood was spread wide and it looked rather dark and sinister. Then it slithered out of the basket completely and sat on the ground with its head in the air.

The music stopped. The snake turned and looked at them with little glittering eyes.

'I think he's got his eye on you,' said Brian.

Dougal backed away behind Ermintrude.

'Very interesting,' he said.

The Indian looked at them and held the pipe out in this hand.

'He wants to know if anyone would like to have a go,' said George.

'Go on, Dougal!' said Florence.

'Yes, go on, Dougal!' they all said.

'Who, me?' said Dougal. 'Not likely!'

'Go on,' they shouted, 'don't be a spoil-sport.'

'I'm not spoiling anyone's sport,' said Dougal. 'You have a go, if you're so keen.'

'I don't think ladies are allowed to,' said Florence.

'And I'm too small,' said Brian.

'And Dylan's asleep,' said Ermintrude.

'So that leaves *you*,' they said.

They pushed Dougal forward. He went very reluctantly.

'All right! All right! Don't push!' he said.

The Indian gave him the pipe. Dougal looked at the cobra nervously. He gave a little toot. The cobra stayed quite still. Dougal gave another little toot and then blew very hard as the cobra came a little way towards him. The music Dougal played was quite unearthly, but the cobra raised itself and swayed to and fro.

It came a little closer to Dougal.

'If you think that's charming I've got news for you,' it hissed.

Dougal stopped playing.

'I'm doing my best,' he whispered. 'I'm not used to this, you know.'

'Well, don't blow so hard,' said the cobra, 'and we'll all enjoy ourselves more.'

Dougal played less hard. The cobra swayed and slithered.

'That's much better, boyo,' it said, and when Dougal gave a final little toot it disappeared into the basket.

Everyone applauded.

'You were wonderful, Dougal,' said Florence. 'I didn't know you could charm snakes.'

'Neither did he,' said Brian, quietly.

'What?!' said Dougal.

'Nothing,' said Brian.

They thanked the snake-charmer, woke Dylan up and went on. In another part of the square there was a large crowd. They went across to have a look. Another Indian in a turban was playing a pipe and in front of him was another basket.

'Another snake-charmer?' said Florence.

'Just watch,' said George.

The Indian played his pipe, and as he did so a small boy started to twirl and dance in front of him. He twirled and twirled and leapt and leapt. Finally he put his hand into the basket and pulled out – a long coil of rope.

'That's a funny looking snake,' said Dougal.

'Just watch,' said George.

The pipe played and the boy whirled some more, this time twirling the coil of rope round and round. Then he threw one end of it into the air with a great shout and stood quite still. The pipe stopped playing. There was silence.

*The rope didn't fall back to the ground.*

It stayed stretched up into the air even though there was nothing to hold it. It was as though someone had attached it to a hook in the sky.

'Gracious,' said Florence.

'Just watch,' said George.

The pipe started to play again, and the small boy took hold of the rope and pulled. It stayed where it was. The pipe played some more and the boy began to climb the rope. Up and up he went, right to the top; the pipe stopped playing, the rope fell to the ground and the boy landed on his feet beside it.

Everyone applauded and cheered like anything.

'I don't believe it,' breathed Florence.

'No, not many people do,' said George.

'I want to have a go! I want to have a go!' said Brian. 'I want to have a go at the rope trick!'

Everyone laughed and laughed, but Brian was allowed to have a go.

'Can my friend play the pipe? he asked.

The Indian nodded and handed the pipe to Dougal.

'You'll never do it,' he said to Brian. 'Stop being such a great clump.'

'Just play,' said Brian. 'We snails are very deft in our own way.'

Dougal sighed and started to play the pipe. Brian whirled and whirled, squeaking with delight. He disappeared into his shell.

'Sorry,' he said, coming out again. 'I didn't mean to do that.'

'Oh, get on with it,' said Dougal.

Brian whirled some more, got hold of the rope in his mouth and with a great squeak threw it into the air. It went up and up, and then came down again and coiled itself over Brian, covering him completely.

Dougal nearly swallowed the pipe with laughter.

'Why's it gone dark?' said Brian, in a muffled voice.

Florence uncoiled the rope from Brian.

'I don't think you got it quite right,' she said.

Brian looked at Dougal suspiciously.

'Were you playing the right tune?' he asked.

'How should I know?' said Dougal.

'Well, try again,' said Brian.

They tried again. Dougal blew and blew, and Brian threw the rope up again with a shout.

It stayed there. It was not quite straight. In fact it looked a bit like steps made of rope, but it stayed there.

'I've done it!' shouted Brian, and he started to go up the steps.

'Careful, Brian!' called Florence.

Brian reached the top and stood there.

Everyone applauded and cheered. Brian gave a great shout of triumph – and disappeared.

There was silence.

'He's disappeared!' whispered Florence.

The crowd began to murmur in wonderment.

Ermintrude went over to the rope and looked up.

'He's certainly not there,' she said. 'Wherever can he have got to?'

'Try playing a tune, Dougal,' said Florence.

Dougal sat in silence looking up at the rope.

'Dougal!' said Florence again. 'Try a little tune.'

Dougal didn't seem to hear. A tear rolled down his face.

'My little chum,' he sniffed. 'Gone, and never even said good-bye. I should never have let him try it. I'm a beast!'

And he burst into tears and buried his head in the basket.

'Now, Dougal,' said Florence, 'this isn't being any help at all.'

'He didn't even take a lettuce with him,' wailed Dougal. 'He'll get hungry!'

And he buried his head in the basket again.

'Dougal!' said Florence. 'Pull yourself together.'

Dougal wailed louder then ever.

'My little perky friend,' he moaned, 'he's left me all alone.'

'Not quite alone, dear thing,' murmured Ermintrude. '*We're* here.'

'It's not the same,' howled Dougal, and buried his head in the basket again as Brian popped his head out of it.

'Evening all!' he said, laughing.

'Brian!!' said Florence, hugging him. 'We thought we'd lost you.'

'Oh, you did give us a turn, you naughty thing!' said Ermintrude.

'Sorry,' said Brian.

He turned to Dougal.

'Hello,' he said.

Dougal looked at him for a long moment.

'Snail,' he said, 'I'll give you a count of three to get out of that basket and out of my sight, you great blundering disappearing OAF, YOU!!!! ONE!'

Brian got out of the basket.

'Did you miss me?' he said.

'TWO!' said Dougal, threateningly.

'Why's your face all red?' said Brian.

'THREE!' said Dougal, and he leapt at Brian and chased him into the crowd.

Everyone cheered and hooted.

'You know, I think they're quite fond of each other really,' said Ermintrude.

'Of course they are,' said Florence, 'but I wonder how Brian did that trick?

There was a 'bong' and Zebedee landed beside her.

'Zebedee!' said Florence. 'I might have known!'

'Just dropped in to see how you were getting on,' said Zebedee. 'Everything going all right?'

'We're having a wonderful time,' said Florence.

There was a screech and Brian hurtled back into the square followed by Dougal.

'Stop it, you two,' said Florence, 'Zebedee's here.'

Dougal slithered to a halt in a cloud of dust and

looked at Zebedee.

'Ah! I might have known,' he said. 'It was *you*, wasn't it?'

'I like to keep my hand in,' said Zebedee, 'and it's a long time since I made a snail disappear up a rope.'

'No, not something one does every day,' said Ermintrude, thoughtfully.

'Well, I wish you'd do it again,' grumped Dougal.

'Now, Dougal,' said Florence, 'you know you don't mean that.'

'You don't mean it! You don't mean it!' shouted Brian.

Dougal sat on him.

'Having good weather back home?' he said to Zebedee, chattily.

'Tolerably,' said Zebedee, 'thank you. Which reminds me, I must be off again. Glad you're having a good time.'

And he bonged away.

'Now, Dougal,' said Florence, 'get up off Brian and come along. It's time to go.'

Dougal got up. 'Oh, hallo!' he said to Brian. 'I didn't see you there.'

'I shall forgive you,' said Brian slowly, 'because I am high-minded and lovable, but there are times when you go too far.'

'Oh, come on,' said Dougal, 'or we'll miss the carpet and I don't want to be stuck in India with *you*.'

They all got back on to the carpet and rose into the air again, waving good-bye to everyone left in the square.

'Now which way shall we go?' muttered George to himself. 'Which way?'

A huge bird flapped slowly along beside them. It was a vulture.

'What's the traffic like over Burma, Elsie?' shouted George.

'Oh, my dear,' said the vulture, 'you know what Burma's like this time of the year.'

'Bad?' said George.

'Like Southend on August Bank Holiday,' said Elsie.

'Thank you,' said George.

'You're welcome,' said Elsie, and she flapped slowly away.

'We'll go the long way round,' said George. 'Elsie always knows,' and he turned the carpet and flew northwards.

'What *I* want to know,' said Dougal darkly, 'is how a vulture from India knows about Southend.'

'I expect she pops over there for a piece of rock,' said Brian.

'You'll get a piece of rock if you're not careful,' said Dougal. 'Right on the bonce.'

'Dougal, don't be vulgar,' said Florence.

She looked down. They were flying over some very high mountains covered in snow.

'Oh, how beautiful,' she breathed. 'Look!'

They looked.

'Himalayas,' said George, briefly. 'Mount Everest on the left.'

He looked down and waved. Away in the distance, almost on top of the highest mountain in the world, was a furry figure. It waved back.

'Friend of yours?' they said.

'Sort of,' said George.

'What's his name?' they said.

'Yeti,' said George, and he turned the carpet north-wards, leaving the mountains far behind.

# North Pole

When they woke up again they were in what seemed to be a very strange place. The light was very bright and white, and there was nothing but snow and ice as far as the eye could see.

George was sitting on the front of the carpet wrapped in a huge padded jacket with just the tip of his nose showing.

'You'll need your parkas,' he said, pointing to a huge pile of grey clothes.

Everyone put on a parka. They were all like the one George was wearing – padded and warm and with hoods to put over the head. Brian's was a bit like a sleeping bag so he got inside.

'Will someone pull it tight round my neck?' he asked.

'With pleasure,' said Dougal, and he pulled with his teeth at the cord round Brian's neck.

'Eeek!' said Brian, going purple. 'Not so tight!'

'Sorry,' said Dougal, fiendishly.

Ermintrude slung her parka over her back and popped the hood over her head.

'I don't really feel the cold,' she said, 'but I suppose it's as well to be *prepared*.'

George said they would go and have some breakfast when they were all ready.

'I've got some transport laid on,' he said.

'Can't we take the carpet?' said Florence.

'No anti-freeze,' said George briefly, 'but I'll be here when you get back.'

'Oh, right,' they said.

'Here it comes,' said George, and across the ice came a large sledge pulled by seven huge dogs.

Dougal went quite pale.

'I say,' he said faintly, 'I hope you don't expect *me* to do that, do you?'

The sledge came to a halt in a flurry of snow and six of the dogs lay down on the ice, panting. The seventh, and biggest, came across to the group.

'Hello, Pixie,' said George.

'*Pixie!!?*' hissed Dougal.

The sledge-dog growled hallo at George and came across to Dougal.

'So you're the new boy, eh?' he snarled, showing a great many teeth.

'Well . . . er . . . not exactly,' said Dougal. 'I mean . . . I . . . er . . .'

'I was told there was a sledge-dog here, so I only brought six of the boys,' said Pixie. 'Union rules calls for eight. So are you or aren't you?'

'Oh yes, he is!' squeaked Brian. 'He's been looking forward to it!'

'Be quiet!' hissed Dougal.

Pixie went back to George.

'Got a bit of trouble here,' he said. 'Can't move without eight dogs.'

'He says he can't move without eight dogs,' called George.

'Well, he moved here with seven,' shouted Dougal.

'Special circumstances,' growled Pixie.

'Special circumstances!' shouted George.

Dougal groaned.

'I think I can see how this is all going to end up,' he said.

'Do it for us, Dougal,' said Florence.

'Oh, wheedle, wheedle!' muttered Dougal.

'Think of the experience,' said Brian.

'I *am* thinking,' said Dougal, 'and that's just the trouble.'

'Think of breakfast, Dougal,' said Florence.

Dougal groaned again.

'Oh, all right!' he said. 'What do I do?'

Everyone got on the sledge while Pixie harnessed Dougal to a long line. All the other dogs looked at Dougal with interest.

'When I say "MUSH", you pull,' said Pixie.

'MUSH!?' said Dougal. 'Is that absolutely necessary?'

'Union rules,' said Pixie.

He went to the end of the line, winking at the other dogs. They all nodded back.

Dougal turned.

'Keep your eyes strictly to the front!' snarled Pixie.

'I know! I know! Union rules!' muttered Dougal, fixing his eyes firmly to the front.

'MUSH!' barked Pixie, and Dougal pulled. As he did so the other dogs quietly stood to one side and as Dougal hauled at the sledge they all got on, winking at each other.

'MUSH! MUSH!' shouted Pixie, and Dougal pulled and pulled.

On board there were great hissings and splutterings of laughter.

'We always do this to someone new,' giggled one.

'It's a trick we have,' they hooted.

On the end of the long line Dougal pulled and panted.

'Union rules,' he grumbled. 'Huh!'

They came to a large log cabin.

'Whoa!!' shouted Pixie, and Dougal stopped thankfully.

'You can turn round now,' they shouted, and Dougal turned and looked. Everyone was sitting on the sledge laughing like anything.

Dougal looked at them.

'I suppose you think that's very funny,' he said.

'Are you very tired, Dougal?' said Florence, anxiously.

'Oh, no!' said Dougal, sarcastically. 'I've just pulled about fourteen tons of dead weight a hundred miles across the ice – why should I be tired?'

Florence put her arm round him.

'Come and have some breakfast,' she said. 'I'm sorry they played a trick on you.'

'I quite enjoyed it actually,' said Dougal.

So they went to have some breakfast, leaving Pixie and the others hooting with laughter in the snow.

'Uncouth lot,' muttered Dougal with dignity.

Inside the hut breakfast was being prepared by some creatures completely covered in white fur. One, the biggest, was at a large stove cooking something. Another, not quite so big, was laying the table, and a third, quite small, was setting out chairs. They were polar bears.

'Porridge?' said the biggest one.

'Er . . . that would be lovely,' said Florence, nervously.

'Kindly sit down then,' said the middle-sized one.

'Not there!' shouted the little one, just as Dougal was about to sit down.

Dougal leapt up.

'That's my chair!' said the little one.

'Sorry,' muttered Dougal, sitting somewhere else.

'*You* can sit in my chair,' said the little one to Florence.

'Thank you,' murmured Florence, sitting.

'It's just that we did have some trouble once before,' whispered the middle-sized bear, 'and he's never forgotten it.'

Ermintrude sat in the biggest chair and it collapsed under her with a crash.

The biggest bear turned slowly at the stove.

'It's happened again, Mother,' he said.

'I'm afraid it has, Father,' was the reply.

'I'm very sorry,' said Ermintrude, faintly.

'That's all right,' sighed the bears.

Everyone had some porridge, and when they had finished they thanked the bears and went outside.

Pixie and the others were waiting.

'Want to go to the North Pole?' they said.

'Not if I've got to pull,' said Dougal, grimly.

'Not this time,' they assured him and everyone, including Dougal, sat on the sledge while Pixie and the others harnessed themselves up.

'You know, mam, those bears remind me of something,' Dylan said to Florence.

'I was just thinking the same thing,' said Florence.

'Good porridge though, wasn't it?' said Brian, happily.

'Too hot,' growled Dougal, and they were off, travelling very fast across the ice with Pixie in the lead and Brian standing on the front of the sledge shouting 'MUSH' with all his might.

They came to a halt after a while and the dogs lay down on the ice, panting.

'Here we are,' said Pixie.

They all looked around. There was nothing to be seen.

'Here we are, where?' said Brian.

'North Pole,' said Pixie.

'I can't see an Eskimo, let alone a Pole,' giggled Dougal.

'I think there should be a Pole of some sort,' said Ermintrude, 'otherwise it doesn't seem quite fair to anyone who's come all this way.'

'Well, it's always been like this,' said Pixie.

Ermintrude looked at him.

'I can see no reason why that means it should *stay* like this,' she said, 'and I, for one, intend to do something about it.'

'What had you in mind, Ermintrude?' said Florence.

'Well, I thought something fairly tasteful in the *flag* line,' said Ermintrude. 'Perhaps one marked "With love from Ermy".'

'That's *tasteful*?' whispered Brian.

'Oh, leave her alone,' said Dougal. 'She'll never find a flag here anyway.'

But Ermintrude had brought her handbag with her and she began to rummage through it.

'Funny,' she muttered. 'I usually have a flag or two with me, just in case, Ah!'

She pulled out of her handbag the enormous pair of bloomers she had bought in Morocco.

'*Just* the thing,' she mooed. 'Now no one will be able to mistake the place. Pixie dear, have you got a pole?'

Pixie growled and had a look on the sledge.

'There's a fishing rod,' he said,

'That will do perfectly,' said Ermintrude, and she made a hole in the ice, stuck the fishing rod in and fastened the bloomers to the top. They made a brave show but were soon frozen stiff.

'It'll be a bold explorer who thaws *those* out,' said

Dougal, and he and Brian giggled away as Ermintrude saluted her new flag and got back on the sledge.

'Come along,' she said. 'Let's go and see something else.'

'Ermintrude, you're wonderful,' said Florence.

'I know, dear,' said Ermintrude, and they went off to see something else.

Pixie and the others pulled them across the ice.

'Where do you want to go?' they called.

'Anywhere you like,' shouted Florence, so they went on until they came to a low, round building.

'What's *this*?' said Dougal.

'Igloo,' said Brian.

'I beg your pardon?' said Dougal.

'Igloo,' said Brian. 'It's an igloo – that's what it's called, an igloo. Igloo . . . ig . . . '

'All right, all right!' said Dougal. 'I think we have the general idea.'

They all got off the sledge and went across to the igloo. There was a little notice on the outside.

'BIG JANE'S PLACE' it said. 'ALL WEL-COME. ICE-CREAM A SPECIALITY.'

And just underneath was an arrow pointing straight down.

'Where's the door?' said Dougal.

'I suppose that arrow is pointing to it,' said Dylan, yawning.

'Just woken up?' said Dougal.

'Like . . . this minute,' nodded Dylan.

Brian gave a little squeak.

'In here!' he said, and they looked just in time to see Brian disappearing into a little icy tunnel. Dougal peered into it.

'He's gone!' he said.

'We'd better follow,' said Florence, getting down on her hands and knees and crawling into the tunnel.

'After you, rabbit,' said Dougal.

'Thank you,' said Dylan.

'I don't think I'm going to be able to manage it,' said Ermintrude.

'We'll send you some out,' said Dougal, crawling in.

'Hay flavour, if they have it,' called Ermintrude after him.

Inside it was quite light and cool, and surprisingly big. Brian and Florence were sitting on stools licking ice-creams.

'Hey, it's great!' said Brian.

Dougal and Dylan looked around.

There were lots of little tables and a long low counter with tubs of ice-cream on it. Behind the counter was a large lady.

'What's yours, boys?' she drawled.

'Er . . . tutti-frutti, mam,' said Dylan.

She looked at Dougal.

'You don't have tea, by any chance?' he said.

'TEA!!?' said the lady. 'TEA!!!?'

'It doesn't matter,' said Dougal hastily, 'just give me what he's having.'

And he pointed to Brian.

The lady passed over a dish. Dougal took a big lick.

'Errgh!' he said.

'Carrot flavour,' said Brian, happily. 'Can't beat it.'

'Errgh!' said Dougal again.

'Something wrong, Mac?' said the lady, dangerously.

'Oh no . . . er no! Delicious,' said Dougal, and he took another little lick.

'That's typical of *you*,' he hissed at Brian.

'I can always be relied on,' said Brian, beaming.

There was a grunting noise from the tunnel and a huge man with a white beard came in.

'Evening, Jane,' he said. 'Usual, please.'

Jane passed him over a dish of ice-cream.

'How's business?' she said.

'Oh, so-so,' said the man, 'just coming up to the rush. Always the same around Christmas.'

He threw back his coat and they saw that underneath he was dressed entirely in red.

'Hey!' said Dougal. 'Aren't you . . . ?'

'Hush, Dougal!' said Florence, quickly.

The man turned to Dougal.

'Were you addressing me?' he said.

'Er . . . no,' said Dougal.

The man finished his ice-cream, buttoned up his coat and left.

'Hey,' whispered Dougal, 'that was . . .'

'I *know*,' said Florence. 'Come along.'

They finished their ice-creams, said thank you to the

lady and crawled outside again.

Ermintrude was standing with a dreamy look on her face.

'I've seen him!' she sighed. 'Oh, I've seen him!'

'Who?' said Dougal.

'*Him*!' said Ermintrude. 'Look!'

And away in the distance they saw another huge sledge drawn by six reindeer disappearing into the distance.

'I knew it was him!' said Dougal. 'Why wouldn't you let me ask him?'

'I don't think Father Christmas likes to be disturbed when he's working,' said Florence.

'That's not what they told me at Harrods,' said Brian.

'The North Pole is different,' said Florence. 'Come along.'

And they all got on the sledge and went back to the carpet.

'Had a good time?' said George.

'Marvellous,' said Florence. 'We've seen all sorts of things.'

'And all sorts of *people*,' said Ermintrude, dreamily. 'I wonder if he'll remember me?'

'We planted a flag at the North Pole,' said Brian.

'Flag?' said George. 'Union Jack?'

'Not *exactly*,' said Ermintrude, as they got on the carpet and rose into the air.

They flew out over the ice. Travelling in the same direction was the man on his big sledge drawn by six reindeer. George went past him.

'Busy?' he called.

'Will be come Christmas,' called the man, and they heard him booming with laughter as they flew on southwards.

# *America*

Dougal woke up with a yawn and looked around. He gave a start.

'I don't believe it,' he whispered. 'Look!'

Florence, Ermintrude and Brian looked.

It was Dylan. He was awake and standing up.

'He's awake!' said Ermintrude.

'And standing up,' said Brian.

'Awake *and* standing up,' said Dougal. 'Must be the first time for *days*!'

They all went closer to Dylan. He was standing looking out over a huge prairie. They had landed right in the middle of it, and for miles and miles there was nothing but waving grass.

'Wow!' Dylan was murmuring. 'Wow! Wow! Wow!'

They all looked out and around.

'I don't see anything to "Wow!" about,' said Dougal. 'Where are we?'

'America,' said George. 'Texas, I think.'

'Don't you *know*?!' demanded Dougal.

'Not for certain,' said George, 'but see that sign? There'll be a stage-coach along soon and we can ask.'

They looked at the sign. It read . . .

## BURLAP & CO
## STAGING POST

'Oh, I've always wanted to go in a stage-coach,' breathed Florence.

'Well, better have some breakfast first,' said George.

So in between slices of toast and listening to Dylan say 'Wow!' they waited for the stage-coach.

'Aren't we having a marvellous time?' sighed Florence.

'Lovely,' said Ermintrude. 'Absolutely lovely.'

They had just finished breakfast when the stage-coach arrived. It was drawn by six bony horses and driven by a man with a big black moustache. He was perched high up on a driving seat holding what looked like several dozen leather reins in his huge hands. Written across the side of the stage-coach were the words:

## BURLAP & CO · TEXAS EXPRESS
## PLEASE HAVE EXACT FARE

'Wow!' said Dylan.

As the horses panted and champed and jingled their harness, the driver got down stiffly and came over to them.

'How do you do?' he said.

'Er . . . tea?' said Dougal.

The driver looked at him.

'Two lumps, please,' he said.

Dougal poured a cup – the driver took it and sipped, his little finger crooked delicately.

'I take it you're all coming?' he said.

'Oh, yes please,' said Florence.

'Where to?' squeaked Brian.

'There's only one place to go around here,' said the driver, 'and that's Drybone.'

'Sounds *lovely*,' said Ermintrude, doubtfully.

George said he'd be waiting for them when they got back, and they all climbed into the coach and sat down.

The driver cracked the reins, and they all waved good-bye to George and set off at a trot across the prairie. Dougal, Brian, Ermintrude, Dylan and Florence bumped about inside hanging on to little leather straps.

'A *real* stage-coach,' said Florence.

'Enjoying it?' shouted Brian.

'Immensely,' said Dougal, hanging on.

They hit a bump and Dougal was bounced up to the roof and down again.

'Immensely,' he said, grimly.

There was a 'whoop!' from behind.

'What's that?' said Florence.

Another 'whoop!'

Ermintrude stuck her head out of the window.

'What is it?' said Florence.

'I can't see anything,' said Ermintrude.

She looked up at the driver.

'What's that whooping, dear heart?' she said.

'Whooping?' said the driver, going quite pale. 'Did you say whooping?'

'That's what it sounded like,' said Ermintrude.

'INDIANS!!' shouted the driver, and he cracked his whip like anything. The coach shot forward very fast, and Ermintrude bounced back inside and landed on Dougal.

'He says it's Indians,' she said.

'It'll be a blessed relief,' said Dougal.

'Oh, sorry, dear dog,' said Ermintrude, getting off.

'Indians,' said Florence. 'How lovely.'

'But they fire bows and arrows at one,' squeaked Brian, nervously.

'Just the arrows, I think,' said Ermintrude.

'Well, that's *enough*!' said Brian. 'Especially if they *scalp* you too.'

'*Scalp*?' said Florence.

'Cutting all your hair off,' explained Brian. Dougal paled.

'What?' he said.

'They're going to have a lovely time with *you*,' said Brian.

'Oh, shut up,' said Dougal.

The 'whoops' got nearer. Florence peeked out of one of the windows. The stage-coach was going very swiftly, but following and catching up fast were the Indians.

'See them?' said Dougal.

'Yes,' said Florence.

'What do they look like?' said Brian.

'Very fierce,' said Florence.

'Oh my!' groaned Dougal.

The Indians caught up with the stage-coach and rode alongside whooping and shouting.

'Wow!' said Dylan.

The driver pulled the coach to a halt, and the Indians drove round and round it in a circle making a great deal of noise.

'All right! All right! All right!' shouted the driver. 'We surrender!!'

'What do you mean, *we*?' screeched Dougal. 'I don't surrender.'

'Oh, you're so brave!' said Brian.

'Are you surrendering?' demanded Dougal.

'Yes,' said Brian.

'Coward,' said Dougal.

'I know,' said Brian.

One of the Indians opened the door, and they all got out and stood in a little group. The Indians prodded them and one of them pulled at Dougal's hair.

'Don't you *dare*!' shouted Dougal.

The Indians gave a great shout and started to dance round Dougal, waving their bows and arrows.

The driver got down and came across to the others.

'They seem to have taken to my chum,' said Brian.

'Yes, I was afraid they would,' said the driver.

'Afraid?' said Florence.

'They've chosen him to be our champion,' said the driver. 'They'll have a contest. If your friend wins they'll let us go, if not . . .'

He paused.

'Yes?' said Brian.

'I'd rather not talk about it,' said the driver.

'What do you mean?' said Florence, aghast.

'You'll see,' said the driver.

Dougal came across to them carrying a bow and arrow.

'It's all right,' he said, airily. 'They just want to play games. They've invited me to have a little contest, so I suppose I'd better indulge them.'

'But, Dougal . . .' said Florence.

'Sh!!' whispered the driver. 'Better not tell him.'

'Tell him *what*?' said Florence.

'You'll see,' said the driver.

The Indians came over and pointed to a rock some way away. One of them took a bow and shot an arrow into the ground quite close to it. Then they pointed to Dougal.

'My turn?' said Dougal, laughing. 'Certainly!'

'Have you ever fired one of those bow and arrow things?' said Brian.

'No,' said Dougal, 'but I've read all about Robin Hood. He was British, you know.'

'Yes, I know,' said Brian, 'and he was also a dab hand with the old bow and arrow.'

'Oh, stop niggling,' said Dougal. 'I shall need your help.'

'Not likely,' said Brian.

'Snail!' said Dougal, sternly. 'Come here at once.'

'Under protest,' said Brian.

Dougal fastened the bow across Brian's horns, put an arrow in the string and pulled backwards with his teeth.

There was a twang and Brian somersaulted over Dougal's head and landed some way away.

'Oh really!' said Dougal. 'Really!! Can't you hold still?'

'I'm only little,' said Brian.

'Oh, don't be so pathetic,' said Dougal.

He fastened the bow and arrow again.

'Dig your heels in,' he said.

'I haven't got any heels,' shouted Brian.

'Well, dig *something* in,' said Dougal. 'Ready?'

'I suppose so,' sighed Brian.

Dougal pulled the bowstring again.

'I'm slipping!' screeched Brian.

'Hold on, Brian!' shouted Florence.

Dougal pulled some more. Brian started to slip backwards. Dougal pulled harder. Brian slipped further, and they both started to move backwards quite fast.

Dougal let go. The arrow went straight up in the air, and Brian shot towards the rock and landed on top of it with a shout. The arrow came down, hit the bowstring, shot forward and stabbed through the middle of Brian's hat.

'I say!' said Ermintrude.

The Indians gave a great shout and clustered round Dougal.

'We win, I think,' he said modestly, and was about to get back in the coach when the Indians dragged him away again.

'We make you chief,' they shouted.

'I say!' said Ermintrude.

Dougal was presented with a huge feathered head-dress and a tomahawk. He looked very imposing.

'Chief Shaggy-breeks,' whispered Brian.

'We'll have less of that,' said Dougal, 'unless you want to find yourself hairless.'

'I'm already hairless,' said Brian.

'I'll think of something,' said Dougal.

'What are you going to call yourself?' said Florence.

'I think Chief Greatest-Dog-that-Ever-Lived would be quite suitable,' said Dougal, modestly.

'Wow!' said Dylan.

They all got back in the coach and the Indians escorted them to the town of Drybone shouting a lot all the way.

'Noisy little bunch, aren't they?' said Brian.

'Choose your words, snail,' said Dougal. 'We Indians are very sensitive.'

In the town they all had something to eat and then went for a look around. There wasn't much to see as the town wasn't very big, so they walked up and down the main street so that everyone could see Dougal in his head-dress. Not that there were many people about. For some reason as soon as Dougal appeared everyone went indoors.

Except one man. He was very big with a large moustache and a big hat, and what seemed like an awful lot of guns hanging about his person. He stepped into the street in front of Dougal.

'Hold it right there,' he said.

Hold what?' said Dougal.

'You an Indian?' asked the man.

'Yes, he is!' said Brian. 'That's Chief Grated Dog.'

'*Greatest* Dog,' corrected Dougal.

'Oh, sorry,' said Brian.

The man narrowed his eyes and gazed at Dougal.

'I don't like Indians,' he said, slowly.

'Well, that's not our fault,' said Brian. 'What do you want us to do about it?'

'Fight,' said the man.

'Fight?' said Dougal, aghast.

'You'd better be careful,' said Brian to the man. 'My friend is very fierce.'

'Shut up!' said Dougal, fiercely.

'You see!?' said Brian. 'Very fierce.'

'Then he won't mind fighting,' said the man, 'because I don't like Indians.'

'Oh, don't keep saying that,' said Dougal, sharply.

The man leapt back and crouched.

'Draw!' he snarled.

'Oh, he can't draw for toffee,' said Brian. 'He's just fierce.'

'Draw!' said the man again.

'You do meet some funny people,' muttered

Dougal, starting to walk away.

There was a loud bang. Dougal and Brian jumped.

'Where are you going?' drawled the man, holding a gun which was smoking slightly.

'Er . . . we were thinking of having tea,' said Dougal.

'With cake,' squeaked Brian.

'You'll fight first,' said the man.

'We certainly will *not*,' said Dougal. 'We don't approve of fighting.'

'So don't rouse us,' said Brian, 'if you know what's good for you.'

'There's no need to say things like that,' hissed Dougal.

But Brian ignored him.

'My friend is a wizard with the bow and arrow,' he said, 'so be careful if you don't want to find yourself *punctured*.'

'What's he like with a gun?' said the man.

'Great !' said Brian. 'He's the greatest. He can shoot a potato at a hundred yards. Chipped,' he added.

The man looked impressed. He handed a revolver to Dougal.

'Show me,' he said.

'Now look what you've done,' said Dougal. 'What am I supposed to do with this?'

'Shoot a potato at a hundred yards,' said Brian.

'Have you *got* a potato?' said Dougal.

'No,' said Brian.

The man hadn't either. It wasn't something he normally carried apparently.

'Wait!' said Brian, dramatically.

He rushed off down the street.

'Where's he gone?' said the man.

'How should I know?' said Dougal. 'You started all this, remember?'

'There's no need to get tetchy,' said the man.

There was a shout from Brian. He was a long way away down the street and holding something on top of his hat.

'FIRE!' he shouted.

'What?!' shouted Dougal.

'FIRE!!!' screamed Brian.

Dougal held the big revolver in his mouth.

'The things I *do*,' he thought, and he closed his eyes and pulled the trigger.

There was a loud bang and Dougal fell over. Brian came scampering back in triumph. He was holding a potato. There was a hole right through the middle of it.

The man went quite white.

'Er . . . excuse me, stranger . . . er . . . Big Chief,' he said. 'I . . . er . . . didn't mean . . . er. . .'

He backed away and started to run.

'I don't think he'll bother us any more,' said Dougal, airily.

He looked at the potato.

'Where did you find that?' he said.

'Lying around,' said Brian.

'Oh,' said Dougal.

'I made the hole with a stick,' said Brian.

'Oh,' said Dougal.

'I didn't want to take the chance that you might miss,' said Brian. 'I hope you don't mind?'

'No,' said Dougal.

They collected the others and caught the stage-coach

back to George and the flying carpet.

'Where are we going now?' asked Florence.

'Secret,' said George. 'On you get and close your eyes.'

They all got on and closed their eyes. With a 'whoosh' the carpet took off, flew very fast for a little while and then landed again.

'You can open them now,' said George.

They opened them and looked around.

'Where's this?' whispered Florence.

'Yes, where?' said Ermintrude.

'What a crazy place,' said Dylan.

'I think it's Mars,' said Brian.

'It's not Mars, it's home!' shouted Florence.

There was a 'boing' and Zebedee appeared.

'Welcome back,' he said. 'Have a good time?'

Everyone started to laugh. Mr Rusty and Mr MacHenry appeared, carrying a large table between them. On it was a huge tea, with a cake saying WEL-COME BACK in pink icing.

'Isn't it funny we didn't recognise it?' said Florence.

'It's because you expected it to be somewhere else,' explained Zebedee. 'It's nice to have you back.'

'It's nice to *be* back,' they said.

'Where shall we go next time?' said Brian.

'We can recommend Bourne-mouth,' said Mr Rusty.

Dougal took a sip of tea and a mouthful of cake.

'We'll consider it,' he said, happily.

# ABOUT THE AUTHOR

Eric Thompson was born on November 9, 1929 in Sleaford, Lincolnshire, and brought up in the village of Rudgwick in Sussex.

He trained to be an actor at the London Old Vic School and joined the company in 1952 where he met his wife, the actress Phyllida Law. Their daughters, Emma and Sophie are both actors.

A founder member of the Royal Exchange Theatre in Manchester, he directed several plays there, in the West End of London, Washington, Broadway, Holland, New Zealand and Canada.

He first wrote *The Magic Roundabout* from his cottage in Argyll where he hoped to retire with a clinker built boat, a soft-topped jeep and a collie dog. He died in 1982.